THE WAX CHILD

By the same author

My Work
The Employees

THE WAX CHILD

OLGA RAVN

Translated from Danish
by Martin Aitken

VIKING

UK | USA | Canada | Ireland | Australia
India | New Zealand | South Africa

Viking is part of the Penguin Random House group of companies
whose addresses can be found at global.penguinrandomhouse.com

Penguin Random House UK,
One Embassy Gardens, 8 Viaduct Gardens, London SW11 7BW

penguin.co.uk

First published as *Voksbarnet* in Denmark by Gyldendal 2023
First published in English in the United States by New Directions 2025
First published in Great Britain by Viking 2025
005

Copyright © Olga Ravn and Gyldendal, 2023, 2025
Translation copyright © Martin Aitken, 2025

The moral right of the copyright holders has been asserted

Penguin Random House values and supports copyright.
Copyright fuels creativity, encourages diverse voices, promotes freedom
of expression and supports a vibrant culture. Thank you for purchasing
an authorized edition of this book and for respecting intellectual property
laws by not reproducing, scanning or distributing any part of it by any
means without permission. You are supporting authors and enabling
Penguin Random House to continue to publish books for everyone.
No part of this book may be used or reproduced in any manner for the
purpose of training artificial intelligence technologies or systems. In accordance
with Article 4(3) of the DSM Directive 2019/790, Penguin Random House
expressly reserves this work from the text and data mining exception

Set in 11.5/15pt Kepler Std
Typeset by Six Red Marbles UK, Thetford, Norfolk
Printed and bound in Great Britain by Clays Ltd, Elcograf S.p.A.

The authorized representative in the EEA is Penguin Random House Ireland,
Morrison Chambers, 32 Nassau Street, Dublin D02 YH68

A CIP catalogue record for this book is available from the British Library

ISBN: 978-0-241-75274-6

Penguin Random House is committed to a sustainable future
for our business, our readers and our planet. This book is made from
Forest Stewardship Council® certified paper.

A RUMOUR OF WITCHCRAFT

I am a child shaped in beeswax. I am made like a doll the size of a human forearm. They have given me hair and fingernail parings from the person who is to suffer. I was borne by my mistress for forty weeks under her right arm as if I was a proper child, and my wax was softened by her warmth. After this time, she took me to a pastor; it was night, the church was dark and still, and he christened me, the wax child. I was an instrument. This was at Nakkebølle Manor, in southern Funen. My wax mouth cannot be opened.

I know the humans well, though they don't know me. I am an image, in the absence of a child. I have this bottomless, shaft-like longing for the woman who made me, whose name was Christenze Kruckow. Her sweat smelled so tangy, of . . . cloves, perhaps. There were carriages and horses and soldiers. There was marjoram and thyme and rose hip. There were ships that journeyed far across the sea to lay claim to territory. There were ships filled with living bodies in the darkness of their holds. There was a scream. And a refinement. The finest pattern cast by the sun through the grille of the confessional. And through the towns religious processions went, and chorused wonderful song. The year passed, and the years passed. And I was a wax child. I did not age. I lay in the ground and saw it all. Insects and worms approached, to retreat on sensing my poison. I saw the rising of realms, the founding of states, the centralizations of power. I saw the clouds hasten by. I saw the great black tongues of oil advance as the fern from the soil puts out its feelers. I saw hands be raised and clench into fists. I saw knives gleam, children play. I saw steam locomotives, the smallest particle split and exploded. I lay in the ground. And from there, at certain times of the month, I could observe the brilliant moon. No one was carrying me any more.

No one listens to a thing I say. Although I speak all the time. I am a lump of beeswax shaped in the image of a newborn child. I am no more than what may melt and stiffen again in the night. No one comes to me here. I lie and speak with my eyes. My family no longer exists, or rather: my kind of family, a very large one, no longer exists. And still I speak. A steady stream of words that slip from me without cessation, and I too am inclined to think it is often an embarrassment. But I cannot stop it, my mouth will not desist, though I don't know how the words get out – I have no larynx, no vocal band, no tongue. But who does it interest? Children should be seen and not heard, as they say. But then I've already told you, I am not a child, only something that looks like one. Something that longs to be one. I'm an internal event. By nature unfinished, or condemned to anticipation, awaiting my mistress, who since she is dead comes no more. Now I speak again to the soil that covers my face. Now I speak again to the semi-carbonized, the soon-composted apple someone tossed, in the place where I lay.

There was a night when I was still lying in the bed of my mistress. Yes, I remember it. She wakes with a start, sits up, looks out. Others, in the surrounding houses of the town, wake in the same manner. They don't know why. They are possessed by such a strange feeling. I observe them. I hear their thoughts. There's something not right, something awry. The salty air – as if the sea has flooded into their rooms. They don't know it yet, but still they sense it. The Earth turns slowly into modernity. And in the space of an imperceptible moment, the old world has succumbed conclusively to the new.

Whenever a woman nearby to me was about to give birth, I would lie in the ground and feel almost exalted, as if the arrival of every child was a chance for me to find a place in the world, for my soul to dart into one of those newborn infants, my mouth to open and expel its very first cry. But I remained there.

Whenever a woman nearby was about to give birth, a messenger would make haste to the midwife and whoever else the pregnant woman had asked to help. All let go then of whatever was in their hands, and came as quickly as they could. Some in the night, others in the frost of morning; with fleetness of foot they came, and barely inside the door would take upon them the housekeeping. They would introduce a new and temporary regime, which meant that those who normally frequented the house would have to find new places to stay. I saw these women form a ring around the one in labour and lead her to the bath house. I saw them douse the burning-hot rocks with water; I saw the steam and the scalding herbs. They undressed the birthing woman, and the naked one was Anne Bille, the young mistress of Nakkebølle. And by the stone wall of the bath house they had placed me in the ground, and I lay and listened there as Anne Bille gave birth to the first of her children. And the midwife came then with her long strides, known for her skill of directing into another the pains of the woman in labour, and it would be said then that she who received the pain of the travailing woman held the skin girdle. And the women of the household took turns to hold the skin girdle on Anne Bille's behalf. And my own mistress, Christenze, could hold it the longest, and it was said then that this was because she had never lain with a man and therefore possessed a virgin's strength. And later in the morning, Eiler, Anne's husband, returned to the manor, and he stood and kicked at the gravel outside the stone bath house, and said, I heard it myself, to the midwife, that this was a dreadful racket his wife was making in there, and how much could such a thing hurt, and I saw then the midwife's eyes narrow, and without him understanding what was happening she gave him the skin girdle to hold and immediately he fell to the ground and cried, O, help me, I feel such terrible pain, and all the women then laughed, Christenze and Ousse and the others too, they shrieked with laughter, and Ousse said: There, she certainly gave you the skin girdle to hold, that you may learn what your woman endures to bring your offspring to the world.

But every time Anne Bille gave birth, no matter who held the skin girdle, the child died in the days that followed. I heard one of them scream as if death had appeared before it, and soon it expired at Anne Bille's breast, not a single night old. Others were blue and lifeless, too small at birth to survive. Then one day my mistress said to Anne: Anne, I have noticed you are rather unwell. Come to me and I will give you sheep's milk. You have borne four children, and none is alive. Let me help you to keep the next. And my mistress went and milked a sheep. In the kitchen, she took up some of the milk on a spoon and as she heard Anne approach the door she picked from her pocket, with two fingers, a spider and placed it in the milk so that the attercoppe was concealed in it. She stood with the spoon ready when Anne came in, and obediently Anne went to the spoon, put the spoon without a word into her mouth and swallowed the milk and the spider unknowingly in one gulp, and went on her way. At this time she was eight months pregnant and was full of hope and anxiety, and would accept any advice. And when the child came it was alive and well formed, with the correct number of toes and fingers, a girl with chubby cheeks, and Anne sat up in her maternity bed and was radiant, a sigh of relief went out, not only over Nakkebølle, but over all of southern Funen – at last a healthy, bouncing baby was given to Anne, and she swaddled the child. But the next morning the newborn lay cold in her cot. It was Ousse who discovered it, and Anne turned away on to her side in the bed with her back to the child and said nothing. I shall let her be, so you can say goodbye, Ousse said, but Anne did not reply, and Ousse went then to the kitchen, for she was a servant girl, to share the solemn news. And there she sat as yet when Anne came bounding with the child. It lives, it lives! she cried, and held the child out for them to see, and Ousse and Anne bent over the newborn and it was true, the face, with its closed eyes, widened and crumpled, the mouth shaped the smallest of movements, and the lips parted slowly as if to expel a tentative sound. There, you see, Ousse! Anne cried. She lives! And the child's mouth opened and out came not a sound but a spider; and they stood then, as if they were petrified, and gaped at the infant as the spider scuttled across her face and jumped away, and Anne screamed and let go of the child, whose body fell to the stone floor.

And thus some twelve years passed, and before Anne was thirty-two she had given birth to and lost fifteen infants. And with every child that died she became meaner and more bad-tempered, unhappy, abusive, and she would scratch the faces of her servant girls and at dinner would stab her own hand with forks and laugh out loud, and she cast her gaze at Christenze, my mistress, then still younger, though not young, perhaps thirty-six years old, but unmarried, and fond of riding, often at dinner she would still be in riding boots, and Anne scowled then at this ruddy-cheeked, unwed noblewoman and hissed between her teeth: You, 'tis you, you are a witch. But Christenze merely laughed and rolled her eyes and drank more wine, and there were times when Christenze, my mistress, would think it better if she had been born a man, when still a child the thought had struck her that she possessed that very restlessness and strength; and if ever the chance came her way to gallantly step in and perhaps shield in her arms a servant girl who happened for instance to be frightened by a fierce dog at the moat, then the rest of her day would be spent pondering what Christenze understood were manly values, protecting and shielding, riding and fencing. So Christenze had never ingratiated herself to any potential husband, had never married, never wanted to, never felt an urge for mayor or king's lieutenant, nor any marital bed, had shunned all notion of prenuptial agreement, bridal veil and marriage chest, preferring to horse-ride on her own and drink red wine and read letters well into the night; the Beheaded Virgin is what she later would call herself – after death, of course – her head, separated from her body, told me so from within the flames, when they tossed both it and the body, headless, on to the fire, Farewell my child, the lips sighed on seeing me on the arm of another in front of the bonfire, and had I been able to cry my eyes would then have cried, and had my mouth been able to shape a word it would then have done so, but I saw her detached head say: Farewell, my child, farewell from the Beheaded Virgin. However, all this was a long time later. I am anticipating events. Christenze is still alive. It is night, night over southern Funen. She is asleep in her room. She has put me in the basket. The still being of night entwines itself in the treetops. I think I love her with that part of me that is never illuminated.

Whoever wishes to know if a sick person will live or die shall take a gem-stone that is known by the name of emerald and place it then upon a person who is gravely ill. If he is to die, the stone will shatter. It should be placed upon the heart.

Or count how many days from the beginning of his illness and take then a herb having as many leaves as the number of days, and hang it upon the sick person.

Or take the milk of a woman giving breast to a boy and put it in the sick one's urine. Stir, and if the milk runs together, he will become well again.

Or take a crumb of bread and stroke with it the temples of the sick one, then give it to a dog to eat.

Or take a piece of flesh and rub the soles of the sick one's feet with it, and throw then the flesh to a dog. If the dog devours it, this is a sign the sick one will become well again; if the dog does not, then he will die.

A man entered a town hall with an anticipation of total obedience. As a child he was offered the choice between an apple and a knife. He learned how to slaughter a pig. The man I see has access to many castles and manors. He never lives in the same place for any length of time. He is always on his way, administering his realm. He is Christian IV, king of all Denmark and Norway. Mail is read to him. He smells of hidden blood.

She chose the night in which to do it. She lit the fire and began to heat up the water. She saw a shooting star from the window. There was a draught. The beeswax in the pot started melting from the sides. It smelled of honey. When she stirred the pot in order to turn the lumps of wax, it was as if something that at first occupied the darkness surrounding the manor house now had entered the kitchen. She could feel its gaze upon her, a beast such as a wolf, or an elf-creature perhaps – it bit her on the neck. She put her hand to the bite. Two eyes hung before her in the air and looked at her a moment until falling to the ground with a chiming sound as made by flintstones. She searched herself for strength, a love of herself. Tightly she wound a strip of fabric around the mould, and stirred the wax to make sure it was melted. She rubbed some human hair into a knot between her fingers and dropped it into the mould before carefully pouring in the beeswax. The beeswax ran and settled, as inchmeal she poured. And during this procedure her first memory suddenly comes to mind, a recollection she has held inside her, like a lucky pebble or a patch of open water in an ice-covered pond, a recollection to which, many times, she has since returned: She is lying in a bed beside a window. The bedstead is constructed of pale wood, and light is spilling in on her. Outside the window two or three black birds fly with pointed wings. The dark span of the wings is repeated in her mother's dress or long cape, her mother and father are standing over her, about to leave, she cannot remember their faces, only their figures and the sounds their voices made, and that they are speaking about her, but she does not understand their words. They are in a happy mood, and proud, leaving for somewhere. That is all. And now she stands in the kitchen and it is night. No one knows her. I want to give her everything I have. She loosens the figure from the mould. The figure is me. She whispers certain things into my ear. She swaddles me like a child. She tidies up after herself. She removes every trace. She knows certain things about the world. She knows that a rumour of witchcraft pursues her and Ousse. She must be careful. But she knows too that the king will not be so bold as to provoke the nobility at the present time, and that she is protected by her title. There is pleasure in producing me. There is pleasure in the hollow of the night, where a person may be inside the navel of the world.

She fully believed they would never seize her. That she was as invincible as a star. But I saw clearly that a star such as she was a star made of hair, and the hair wound slowly outwards like the shoots of the bindweed, latching on to everything in its path, twisting, sucking the capacity from its surroundings, that it be delivered to its own starry middle, the empty void where wax children live. They will do right to fear me, Christenze thought; but to me my mistress was harmless, as invincible as the foam that tops the wave as it crests into its final peak.

There grew small bluebells along the surrounding wall of Nakkebølle, and in their waists these flowers bore droplets of dew, and it was in these droplets of dew that an exchange in the manor house cellar became preserved, so that I, when once I came into contact with the bluebells' moisture, heard everything. Ousse sat chained to the wall and weeping, and there stood Anne before her and ordered her hatchet-man to pinch Ousse with a red-hot pincer.

Tell me who it is, Ousse, Anne said.

Anne, Anne, Ousse sobbed, as if in the hope of bringing Anne to her senses. Anne, God has given you a terrible cross to bear, that all your children should die so young, but it was never my doing, Anne, I have done nothing.

Pinch her again, Anne said, and the hatchet-man gripped Ousse's thumb with the pincers, and this scream it was that quivered in the droplets of dew. I think that any person who travels to Nakkebølle today and who puts their ear to the dew immediately after it has fallen on the enclosing wall of the manor house grounds may still hear those cries. And now Anne speaks very softly, as if her mouth were very close to Ousse's ear:

Who is it, Ousse? Who kills my children?

God, Anne, it is God, Ousse wailed.

Pinch her again, Anne said. And then: No, Ousse, it is something evil, it can only be Satan. But someone has allowed Satan inside me, to enter my womb. Who is it, Ousse? I know it is you, but who else?

Now there is but a whimper from Ousse, as if she were nothing but a bluebell herself in that cellar, trembling in the wind.

It was you, Ousse, was it not? Good, it is good that you nod. You will go to Heaven now, for confessing your sin. Dear Ousse, I have known you for so long and am quite ill with grief, but I sense how it alleviates that grief for the truth to come out, and that is all I wish. It will do you well to cleanse yourself, so that you may receive the forgiveness of God, this is a good thing, and my inquisitor here shall be my witness, but make sure to expel it all, Ousse, for you must stand cleansed before your God, you must be cleansed of your sin, there must not be a single smudge left upon you, if He is to take you. So I must ask you one last time, Ousse, and now you must answer me honestly, otherwise I shall be compelled to order him to heat up the iron again. Because you do understand, do you not, that I have become wise to your having lied to me the whole time, that you are one of the reasons I have been subjected to all this pain? But I forgive you, Ousse, for I know you were seduced by another, a devious serpent I have nourished at my breast in this house and called my friend, and that person is Christenze, is it not, Ousse? It is Christenze who is behind it all, is it not? She has hated me for being married while she has remained unwed; because she has no money, although she is noble. And because she is ugly, even if she cannot help it, still it has made her believe that she deserves better, and now I see, Ousse, that she is behind it all, and no doubt has threatened you into silence; indeed, she must have done, so do not feel badly about it, Ousse, you have merely been an instrument in the wrong hands, and God and everyone else will forgive you when the name of your evil mistress passes your lips. My dear friend, do you remember when we picked the flowers of the field on Bartholomew's Day and swore that we would always be true to each other? It is Christenze, is it not? You nod. Open your lovely eyes so that I may see my Ousse of old. Yes, the tears of relief now run upon your cheeks. Fear not, for as truly as once I took your hand in mine on that meadow, I shall make sure Christenze is duly punished.

Within the labyrinth of pleasant smells and pale green pent roofs where my mistress walked was a taste of alkaline, of chloroplasts and perfume. In one hand she carried Eiler and Anne's summons, in the other a letter of her own composition that she would request be read out to the court on her behalf. She was not intending to be there herself. She does not think about Ousse, and will not. She does not think about Ousse's swollen eye that looked at her through a hole in the stone wall. She does not think about Ousse's mouth, puckered as a knot in a rope. She does not think about the stupid tear that trickled down Ousse's filthy cheek. She does not think about Anne, nor about Anne's soft and ever cool hands when, always, they would clasp Christenze's face in gladness on her return from horse-riding. She does not hear their laughter, her hand does not recall the cloth she pressed against Anne's flesh that it would not be torn open; she does not think about that time they found an ancient coin in the bleaching field and were excited at their discovery. She does not think about the king, nor does she think about tar; she does not think about her own tongue and its yearning for the scream. She grinds her teeth until a sliver of one comes away and unwittingly she swallows it, eats of her own skeleton.

This man, I see him, by the name of Eiler Brokkenhuus, master of Nakkebølle Manor, who requests a
thing-witness, an assembly of eight good men to be
convened at Salling hundred court in the month of May
1615, wishing thereby to initiate proceedings against
my mistress with the charge that she did harm by the
means of witchcraft his wife Anne Bille, thereby causing
her to have lost her children; I see how, in the bead of
perspiration that trembles upon the bow of his upper lip,
a bare oak tree is reflected, as my mistress's closest male
relative, her cousin Jens Axelsen of Årslevgodt, reads to
the court her written reply: Since you, master of Nakkebølle Eiler Brokkenhuus, and you, mistress of that house
Anne Bille, have summoned me, these words shall be my
reply to the mendacious accusation made with diabolical intervention by Ousse Lauritzens against my person.
How, in the presence of God, can you justify the manner
in which you now act towards me, an innocent, impov-
erished victim of untruth? I, who for so many years have
toiled in your house like the poorest of servant girls. Can
you, or anyone else, say to me in all honesty that I have
concerned myself with witchcraft, such as you claim on
the grounds of Ousse Lauritzens having confessed it?
I will remind you, Anne Bille, of what you said of your
unfortunate birth when I sat with you on the edge of
your bed, and fed you before you rose: you said then
that you were not hurt as much by giving birth to dead
infants than by the thought that others believed that
you had been poisoned or were yourself the reason for

them dying. And you said too that the doctor Cornelius had told you the reason for your losing the child the first time you gave birth. The same reason without doubt that you lost all the others too. I know that truth, yet am not inclined to reveal it here.

I wish only to be made as leprous as Naaman, as cursed as Judas, if all that is written about me in the confession of Ousse Lauritzens is not demonstrably the clearest and most obvious lie. May God give that all who have concocted these accusations against me stand with shame and scaling hearts. Here said and written at Bellinge, this seventh day of the month this present year.

I see the king with the smell of the eye. The wind travels far; across the bay alone with this vision. He is impelled to issue a commandment. Listening, I hear time as a clearing among trees, where cattle graze freely; and I hear the eye when later it is crushed like a fruit of slime beneath a hoof. The eye belongs to a cobbler, a smith, a baker, one who calls himself a theologian, good citizens, king's lieutenants, noblemen, a bishop. A diamond-shaped amulet of jade hangs around the king's neck and he fingers absently the finely cut stone while the matters of the day are presented to him. A society of witches has been exposed in Funen. Someone from Nakkebølle has sent him Christenze Kruckow's written speech. A notary reads it aloud to the meeting. It is the first time he hears her name.

Take a swallow bird. Take her heart and roast it on a stick. Take then the swallow's tongue and place it underneath your own. Eat then the swallow's heart. Carry with you thereafter the swallow's tongue, and whenever someone is angry with you place the swallow's tongue underneath your own and speak to the person who is angry and her anger towards you will at once be stilled.

And so Christenze was done with southern Funen, she left Ousse to the bonfire, packed her wadmal skirt and her medallions and her house altar with its image of the Virgin Mary and did not look back, wanting only to escape the rumour that clung to her, and when the carriage trundled out from Nakkebølle's courtyard, the gravel crunching beneath its wheels, Anne's scream was heard far across the fields; but underneath Anne's scream Christenze heard another, and it was I who screamed, wordlessly, in the soil in front of the stone house, without opening my mouth I screamed, and as a whistle sounds in the ear of a dog, my mistress heard me, Wait, she said to the driver, and jumped out and ran back, it was imperative that she not be discovered, and yet she ran to where I lay and scrabbled in the earth to exhume me, and had my eyes been able to weep I would surely then have wept when she whispered, Good morning, brushed the dirt from my beeswax face, tucked me away under her skirts and ran back to board again the carriage and speed away to North Jutland. The year was 1615 and soon the king would send his ships to India. She was without money and unmarried. Her only child was me. I snuggled against her thigh, I breathed in the detail of her smells, I heard the bell-tower sound.

I saw the low-slung hills, Rold Forest, Rebild Bakker, Aalborg. I saw, between the trees as we rattled past, a big heart, closing. Christenze was occupied by considerations unknown. I kept my thoughts on the moon. Cold, long nights in the red glow of the fireplace. From the town and its environs: a sense of scale. From the dead through the years: a sense of scale. I saw ships arrive, drunken folk fall into the harbour. I saw buildings be erected, lanterns suspended in the streets at Christmas. I saw goldsmiths' stalls and sheeny lemons in wooden crates. Now and then, I turned my back on progress. Everything throws, when entering the path of the sun, a shadow. Time too has its shadow, the ages of man and what the poets call the spirit of the age have shadows, and I saw them hurry across Aalborg, in the great perspective of things a large and a small town all at once, a pearlescent kitchen midden. The passage of the spirit of the age is long and laborious, some four hundred years I have seen, and now it turns on to its opposite side, the great serpent in its corridor-shaped nest, the times are changing. The wheel revolves, old ideas are swept away and trampled underfoot, soon you shall all be crushed. And Christenze looked for friends. In one of her dreams she came to me and said she was afraid of her body. But when awake she was as ever fearless, and I was her mending and received all needles.

I saw in the night cats leave the church in droves, I saw them conduct themselves with swine in the street, and I saw the gravedigger in the churchyard puff on a cabbage pipe; I saw in a single vision the town's fleas in all their thousands, I saw blood in small and large quantities, I saw barley porridge and the insipid salt herring. I saw funeral pyres and body parts displayed on the square as a deterrent. I saw money change hands and land be parcelled out, I saw humans bought and sold, lace underneath a skirt. I saw brother turn against brother, and mother against daughter. I saw hearts thirst for revenge and hands that craved for violence. This was not Nakkebølle, it was not even Funen; shudders ran even through my hardy wax, this was Aalborg, 1616, city of hate.

And then one day, on the street called Algade, Christenze met Maren. Maren, who, Christenze at once discerned, gleamed with a light that was golden, as though she were part deity, part effervescent ale, and men flocked about her and her long hair, and she laughed at them, and in Maren Christenze sensed a distant region. When they clasped hands in greeting, Maren without hesitation hooked her arm under Christenze's and said, Let me show you around, you're new in town, and they looked into each other's eyes and Christenze there recognized in Maren what neither of them had words for, but which Christenze saw to be a marshland or a hidden room, and Christenze's lips then almost sprang from her face, so badly they wanted to get to Maren's. And secretly Christenze sniffed in Maren's smell and the smell of Maren's hair and Maren's breath, it smelled of milk and salted meat and hay.

They sat in the front room of the house on Kattevad and drank wine, and Maren said, If the Devil comes to you, you must offer him a loaf of rye bread and set him to break it into pieces, and when he cannot he must take his leave. And Maren lifted Christenze's hand, a thrill ran through her, and Maren took a needle and pricked Christenze's finger and allowed some few drops of blood to drip into her wine, and then Maren raised her glass with a radiant smile, whereupon she drained it in a single swallow. And Maren said, I look forward to you meeting the others. And when you come over, come in a dress of white linen, for we will be dressed the same, and on the bib you must embroider a mark with red silk thread. And as Maren drew the sigil on a piece of paper she went on: You must wear shoes of white leather, and you must bring with you a crown made out of virgin paper, and on it, before you come, you must write your name backwards in red ink. And Christenze got up and went towards Maren and smoothed her hand over the neckline of Maren's dress, and they looked at each other, and that was that, all then was lost and won, and from my basket in Christenze's room I cried, but she heard nothing, because now she sat on Maren's lap, and the light on the table, she blew it out.

If you are enchanted by forbidden love of a woman, you must put on a pair of shoes and walk about until the feet sweat. But walk quickly, so quickly that the feet do not begin to smell. Remove then the right shoe and drink from it some ale or wine, and at once all love for her will be lost.

After this, Maren and Christenze would visit each other frequently. And my mistress decided to lend me, her wax child, to Maren. And in Maren's house I lay in a large chest with a whisk of bundled twigs. And every so often Maren would pick me up and move the whisk upon me, patterning thereby my wax with spirals. And I would look up into Maren's face, though she would never look down but keep her eye on the street as she drew the whisk this way and that, and everything about her was pointed and dainty and quivering as the whisk. Occasionally, a girl would come too and lift the lid of the chest to peep inside when no one was looking. Are you a real live child? she whispered then. But I could not answer, could not even blink, and the chest would then be closed again, and because I could see nothing but the lid, I decided to perceive my surroundings with my back, and with my back I heard and saw the Limfjord, the quaysides and the marketplace. I saw the mound with its gallows dripping with rain. I saw a servant girl drown her newborn in secret. I saw the sand of the execution place absorb the blood from the beheading. I saw a breastbone at the bottom of a tub of ale. I saw a goldsmith melt down stolen goods. I saw two children freeze to death on the street. I saw the ships come in with oranges, marzipan and blue raisins. I saw resentments old and new, saw pearls as on a string be spilled upon the cobbles. I saw Maren and Christenze find Elisabeth, wife of the pastor Klyne, weeping in an alley where she sat in the filth and was inconsolable, and Maren took her in and gave her wine to settle her, but the woman just cried and cried, and Maren patted her head gently as one would pat a dog. This is how she has been ever since she got married, she told Christenze. Can I have some more? Elisabeth sniffled, and held out her glass, which Maren filled again. Where is Klyne? Maren asked. Preaching, Elisabeth replied, and drained the glass, then added: Preach is all he does. Are you still having a hard time with each other? Maren asked. A feral look darted in Elisabeth's eyes, like an animal crossing a way, her jaw tightened and she nodded her head. The three women sat and shared the bottle between them, and I saw Klyne in front of the altar in the church raise his arms in the blessing; I saw the bowed heads, I saw the muscles of the neck from within, the gullet as a throat was cleared of phlegm, and I saw the woolly reassuring darkness inside the human bodies, each and every one a blood-red altar sheathed by the pierceable casing of the skin, and they sang without knowing like clusters of wild grape, their chirping came to me as coils of smoke or threads of honey, and together they formed a grand and single chord that rang out across the fjord and mingled with the rush of the waves, the whistle of the wind, the stars' metallic clang. They went through the streets like waves of sound with many eyes, and yet all these people were blind to their own gifts, to their being alive while I was just a doll. My mistress too was blind, and so was the girl who lifted the lid; like absent-minded children they opened their hands and obliviously let them be emptied of life that would never come again.

The preparation of the wool began at the equinox. The carding fests were always in the eventide. There were many women in the town, many girls, and with my mistress I accompanied them through the streets, since one evening they would gather at one place, the next at another, and help each other card the wool. First they would eat waffles and drink mead, then when midnight came a roast would be served, and sweet soup with sago and fruit syrup, and also dried cod. After that they would card again until two or three in the night, depending on how much fleece they had. On the floor between them was a *selde*, a flat wicker basket, that was filled with wool. The oldest among them, who were most practised in the art, would take up a clump and separate it. Canny-eyed, they would hand out a tuft to each of the others, and were so proficient there would always be just enough for everyone, in equal amount. Then they would contest, and the one who finished first would be the ablest. And Christenze would sit in their midst and compete with them while the widest grin was on her face, although she always came last, and if one of them at night encountered an unfamiliar fellow standing in the hall, I would see the others creep quietly through the kitchen to come up behind him and swipe away his hat. And if by chance he happened to keep it, then half a dozen or more would pile on top of him, whereafter he would be obliged to buy it free for a ransom. The carding women would say they had needles and pins to buy for his money. Or I would see how, when such a fellow had come through the door and put aside his hat, they would hide it away so that when he made ready to leave he would not find it, in which case he would have to pay for its return. The children would first be in their beds, but when the fun began they would be up again to watch with gleaming eyes like polished stones from the darkness of the doorway. One night, when it was the turn of Peder Fisker's wife to hold the fest, Peder climbed on to the roof of the house to the chimney and fished up to himself a cup of apple juice with a hook and a line. Before they went home, they would have stewed apples and sheep's milk, and when they made ready to leave, bread would be sliced and handed out, and apples too, and Christenze carried the food in her hands.

They would meet at Maren Knepris's house, a red two-storey building with tarred black half-timbering and a cornice. Between the two wings at the rear was a garden, where Maren grew thyme, marjoram, lettuce and asparagus. In summer they would sit there often, but now it was early winter, and I was the wax child and they picked me up and placed me on the lid of the chest, from where, in the company of the girl, Karen, Maren's daughter, I would watch the grown-ups as if I was a proper child. And now and then Karen would hold a beaker to my mouth and smack her lips and pretend that I was drinking. Harvest came, then there was a topping-out fest, then there was a butchering and sausage-making fest, it was one fest after another. At midnight, the women sat again in the front room and carded their wool and competed against each other. Apelone, Anders Guldsmed's woman, was the quickest each time; it was as if everything about her was quick, her thoughts, her hands, and she had that thing in her eyes, the weight of a wound that will not heal, together with an adamant defiance, a secret that hung about her and drew Christenze magnetically, and then one evening Apelone showed her the knife she carried in her boot, and Christenze gasped. Occasionally, one or two of them would step outside into the night to breathe in the crisp black air, and there Christenze went with Maren and Apelone. In the shifting light from the window that brightened and dimmed with the movements of those inside, Maren draped an arm over Apelone's shoulder and spoke of the time they each were to wed and had sized one another's bridal bed, and Apelone watched Christenze warily.

Who have you got there? she asked Maren, and I heard it all from my place on the chest.

She is one of us, said Maren. Her name is Christenze. You will soon learn to love her. It is very easy.

And there were geese to be plucked, hops to be picked, and the hops were to be kept down, for the plant was vigorous and hardy as any weed, and the small bell-like cones attached like burs to their dresses, there were walls to daub, children to nurse, cheese to make at the whey-celebration, and everything was better, more fun and easier, when you were more than one. There was Mette Pedersdatter, with her long neck. There were Sidsel and Bodil, who came in from Mo. They could card, they could spin, they could ripple and break the flax, they could swingle and scutch it, they could warp and weave. There was Dorte, the oldest of them, whose husband had been so generous as to die at quite the right time, so that Dorte would not be expected to marry again and yet still had much life in her to be lived, and although she was missing an eye and the shadows played on her face as she sat in the corner, she would card at a steady pace with no need to look down, her hands did the work on their own.

And if there was one thing Elisabeth and Dorte could agree on, it was their common annoyance over Elisabeth's husband, the pastor Klyne. Now Dorte complained that Klyne in his sermon had encouraged longer fasting periods and urged that folk go early to bed, moreover that he had moved her further back in the church and that he would no longer come to visit her and eat herring. Elisabeth complained too, and worked herself up to a point of excitement where she believed Dorte had drawn her astray in the conversation, and it was as if then she came to her senses among them and saw that everyone was now laughing at her stupid husband. And so Elisabeth jumped to her feet and made to leave at once, but the women pulled her back and soothed her, and it was the same song and dance again and again: I must go home and pray, she said . . . I have promised my husband to be home early . . . My husband says . . . He will be angry if . . . And in turn they drew her towards them and kissed her, and Elisabeth laughed and cried like a blue tit in their midst.

One spring they sowed the flax. Late in the summer it was harvested and the wispy bundles were retted and broken, hackled and spun. The following spring they wound the yarn into skeins, to be washed and hung to bleach, and during the autumn those among them who were skilled in the craft would weave the cloth. Then came the third spring, and Christenze helped the other women steep and rinse the linen until it was paler. They laid the lengths of fabric out over the bleaching field, laid them there to whiten.

And one of them, Dorte, said: I lost my eye when a horse kicked me in the face, and my cheek felt so strangely warm, and afterwards they said the blood ran as quickly and as quietly as the becks run through the land when the ice melts in spring, and the pain I felt was a place, a room I never knew existed, though still recognized when it opened towards me; somewhere inside me I had known that pain always, known it to be there, even if I had never experienced that my eye should burst, and the horse was calmed, I tasted the wet salty thickness, the sticky plasma in my mouth, and then you came, Maren, and pressed your palm against the strange open window where my eye was, and you pressed as you bade the blood to still: Mary to the streams she went, she held the little Jesus in her arms, and so I still this blood, and so I still the blood in three men's name. And where the blood fell, the others immediately began to turn the soil with the toes of their shoes so the blood was covered, and someone came and took me away, and you, Maren, came with me, you were at my side the whole time, your palm against my injured eye, and the barber-surgeon bandaged half my head; I was forty-eight years old, but when the next day I set out to walk home, I had become ancient, I had become wizen, the children laughed at me, flies buzzed about my bandage, drawn by the smell of the deep-running blood inside my skull; I was a grandam, a grimalkin, a crone, an old ewe and the Devil's milk-wife, I had at once, as if by a stroke of magic, become Dorte Kjærulf, the one-eyed hag.

They have told it many times before. They talk all at once, though no one misses a word. They rise and fall, briskly weaving together the tale as if it was a plait of hair: It was a long time ago. They talked of harmful magic. They talked of how one person was like this, another like that. And there was a man who spoke on the square. A king's lieutenant, it must have been. A lieutenant of the king. Yes, it was Manderup Parsberg. A time when he still was young and only recently come to Aalborg from Germany, where it was said that he had duelled with Tycho Brahe, that it was Manderup who swiped the tip from Brahe's nose, over what they referred to as a *mathematical disagreement*. I remember no more than this. But it was the time when we still used to pick the yellow elf wort in September. No, wait. How was it now? My mother took me out into the field. This was in the south of the country, near Visse. And the pastor rode about and blessed the new-sown wheat. Was that what the harmful magic was? In any case we ceased, we wanted to become better protestants. And there was this other thing too. Remember? Our mothers would make a small incision in the skin to let the sickness out if we had a fever. And then she would say . . . what was it now? No, I've forgotten. But I remember vividly what she would say when one of us got the hiccups. And although my daughters are grown up now, they say it too. I think they have also taught the hiccup rhyme to their own children. Is that what harmful magic is? The thing everyone did to stop the hiccups? Was that heresy? Forgive us. We knew so little about the Devil in those days, now everyone knows so much about him.

Hiccup Miccup Mink
Give me milk to drink
Hiccup Miccup then be gone

There was lead in the kidneys of the king, and warm there. That was how I learned of it, by way of the lead's travelling through the people's blood. He sat and wrote at his desk: Here in Sealand there is much talk of sorceresses in Copenhagen and Elsinore, of which we find a number, and it is only best that they be swept away once and for all, lest our house become infested. These witches have already in several instances sought to make intrusions upon our person. Thanks be to God, they have accomplished nothing, for we are ever vigilant to poor craftsmanship. The Swedes too have endeavoured to inflict harm upon us, and we have discovered in our camp all manner of diabolical arts with wax children set in the ground in numbers, wherefore I must confess to have seen what I have never on any previous occasion seen.

And I was in the king's ear, and I was in the king's mouth, and I was in the king's loose tooth and in the quicksilver of his liver, and did hear. A scratching of the pen across the paper as he repeated the motto of the Crown, *Regna Firmat Pietas* – Piety Strengthens the Realms.

They were together. They set ale and wine upon the table, they set sweetmeats and apples upon the table. Some held hands. One among them touched another's hair and it was like a tongue of water in her hand, her sleek hair and the pleasant smell that rose from the nape of her neck. How was it now with the mistress of Baggesvogn? someone said. Indeed, that good old one, someone said. Have you not heard? someone said. Oh, but then you must. I may have heard it, someone said, but no matter, let me hear it again. Yes, how was it now? someone said. There was a mistress at Baggesvogn, someone said. They called her the mad wife. Yes, every year she lost a bullock, someone said. That was it, yes, someone said. And the lady grew tired of it, someone said. So she made up her mind to ask the Devil why they had to lose so many creatures on their manor farm. Indeed, that part I've never understood. Why would she ask the Devil? Why not a priest? someone said. It's what makes the story so good, someone said. Quiet now, someone said, I want to hear this. But you know it already, someone said. That doesn't matter. No, someone said, what matters is the mistress of Baggesvogn and her livestock. And the mistress of Baggesvogn, someone said, went to the cunning woman. And the cunning woman was the one they called Kirsten Slotved. Her daughter was the pot-wife, someone said. Indeed, someone said. And Kirsten Slotved and the mistress of Baggesvogn, someone said, cast a candle that could be lit at both ends. One end could be extinguished by the Devil, but the other, someone said, only by humankind. Indeed, someone said. Yes, that's it, someone said. Then the mistress of Baggesvogn told her driver to hitch a horse to the carriage, someone said, and told him to take her and Kirsten to the church, someone said. For the old woman had set her claws into the mistress of Baggesvogn, someone said. And when they came to the church it was evening, someone said. And the driver looked on as Kirsten Slotved and the mistress of Baggesvogn went three times around the church, someone said. That's right, someone said, three times around the church they went. And each time they came to the church door, someone said, what did they do? They blew into the keyhole, someone said. They gave themselves over to the Devil, someone said. Oh, dear God, my children, they are ill again, someone said, and now I must go. No, don't go, someone said, it's been such a long time. I wish I could stay, someone said. And I am angry with Mads, someone said. Yes, God, and I am so very tired of Anders, someone said. But what happened to the mistress of Baggesvogn? someone said. I must go, someone said, and went. When Kirsten Slotved and the mistress of Baggesvogn returned to the manor, someone said, they made, can you believe it, a fire in the great hall. Yes, is that not madness? someone said. A fire in the great hall! On account of a bullock! someone said. But something must have given them reason, someone said. It can't have been the creatures it was about, someone said. Do you think it was something else? Yes, there must have been some other reason, something more serious, someone said. Perhaps her husband was ill, someone said, or perhaps it was something else of which she was unable to speak, someone said. Did she have children? someone said. Did she have sisters? someone said. What were her neighbours like? someone said. Was she pursued on the moor by a long-legged black poodle-hound that loped at the side of her carriage whenever she drove, someone said. If she was, it's been missed out, someone said. Either way, someone said. Either way what? What happened then? Yes, what happened? They took a bullock's heart, someone said. Yes, that's right. That was it exactly, someone said. They took the heart from the last bullock into the great hall and were about to put it on the fire, someone said. They locked the doors and lit the candle, for they were going to read from a book, someone said. A bad book, someone said. A black book, someone said. A Cyprianus, someone said. Do not say that word, someone said. I'll say whatever I want, someone said. Anyway, someone said, they read from a certain book. Exactly, someone said, a book they had laid their hands upon. And so it was that they called the Devil to them, someone said and then paused. Yes, now it comes, someone said. Listen now, and listen well, someone said. But they had lit the candle at the wrong end, someone said. Say it isn't true, someone said. But it's as true as the day is long, someone said. What on earth were they thinking? someone said. And without knowing what error they had made, someone said, Kirsten Slotved and the mistress of Baggesvogn called the Devil to them. The Devil himself, someone said. And he came too, someone said. And he blew out the light, someone said. He blew the candle out at one end, someone said. And then it was too dark for them to read, someone said. And then he began to dance, someone said. Indeed, someone said, they danced. And at first the dance was good, someone said. But the Devil was untiring, someone said, and he did dance Kirsten Slotved and the mistress of Baggesvogn to their knees. In the morning, when the servants came, someone said, they saw through the windows that two were sat inside the room, someone said. One sat slumped against the one door, the other against the other, someone said. And the servants had to force open the doors, someone said. Yes, they forced open the doors, someone said, and when they did, someone said, one of the two flopped forward. But it could not be helped, someone said, for how else should they have got in? And then they saw a grisly sight, someone said. What was it? someone said. Yes, what was it? someone said. Ugh, this is the worst of it, someone said. But what was it they saw? someone said. Is there more ale? someone said. Pour me a little wine, someone said. Shall we not step outside for some fresh air? someone said. But what was it? someone said. It was that the women's faces, someone said, had been, well, they'd been gouged, someone said. And something had come out of them and was smeared about the walls, someone said. Ugh, someone said. On the walls? Yes.

Was it their guts? I don't know. Was it pink? I don't know. If it was their guts, it would have been more red. Was it their souls? Smeared about the walls? That part's missed out. But they were dead? Yes, they were dead, and dead they remained. And that was that, yes, that was it, and it was a good one too, someone said.

I was a wax child. I was the servant of my mistress. I was a dragon doll, I was a walnut dropped by a magpie from a great height, the shell split into two as I struck the ground, exposing the kernel. My mistress came into her chamber, she saw me, she took me in her arms. My dearest, I must send you to be my envoy, she said. It was the golden hour; outside the window the sun picked at the tops of the mugwort. Klyne is set upon Elisabeth and there is much tumult, she said. At once I took a she-cat from a corner of the house and together we scurried through the garden across to Elisabeth and Klyne's house. There we found in the bedchamber Klyne standing over his wife, and immediately the cat leapt on to his shoulder and upon its warm feline breath I whispered into Klyne's ear: You must to the church, Klyne, you must to the church at once, if your life is dear to you. Klyne ceased then in his deed and like a sleepwalker turned and made towards the church. To Elisabeth I came now as the cat and licked her fingers, yet she lay unmoving, and tell me why, but we bit her, the temptation was too great, and with the she-cat's tongue I tasted blood, the blood of a pastor's wife, and at home in the basket a droplet appeared on my waxen lip like the merest element in a wine-coloured sea, and my mistress kissed it away, smiled her strange smile, and within her breast there was a howling and yet she held quite still and kept her calm, and without embarrasment she jerked her hand as if plucking a threaded needle from a fabric she was stitching in the air, and at once a droplet of blood appeared suspended and trembling before us, until my mistress then snatched it away in the fist of her hand, and the cat ran home, mirrors moved between the clouds, throwing flashes on to night's ocean; Elisabeth refused to wake, Klyne sat bewildered in the church, they walked separately then and yet would come together, for there was always some feast or revelry, an occasion to be celebrated, somewhere to gather, a day to be marked, a candle to be lit in order that the darkness be kept at bay, and in numbers they would stand in the night and lift each glass to the stars.

It resembled perhaps a cat, but then it got a human head.

It resembled perhaps a cat with a human head, but then, instead of one foreleg and paw, it got an arm and a hand.

It resembled perhaps a cat with a human head and arm, but it got a human shoulder blade.

It resembled perhaps a cat, but then the whole head and upper body were human parts; it was no longer obvious whether the creature would walk or crawl on all fours.

It resembled perhaps a cat, with pink cheeks and a tail; it resembled perhaps me, whom you know so well, although you have forgotten. Since we have spent some small amount of time together, do you remember now?

When they were to clean and gut the herring, they called themselves gill-women. The men who fished would return from the fjord and the wives took up their knives. Fish upon fish would be scraped to remove the slime, then the knife would go the other way to scrape away the scales, then the knife would go the other way again, and then they scraped the neck immediately behind the gills. Close together they would sit, with scarfs to cover their hair; their hands would be red and cold, and the chat would ripple as they removed the guts from the fish. This time they had set me in my place at Karen's side, and so I was present in the guise of a toy. A seal had come after the boat, which the fishermen held to be a glad omen whenever they were at sea.

And you, said Apelone to Dorte, didn't you once talk Elisabeth's Klyne into eating the same herring twice?

He did forget to break the spine on the first one, Dorte replied, and her toothless mouth widened in a grin.

I don't remember that, said Elisabeth.

We're only joking, said Apelone.

No, I don't think so, said Elisabeth, and wiped her hands in her apron.

There was a sniffing of noses and a stamping of feet, it was cold work to sit with the fish.

This will be the last haul of the year, said Maren.

The fattest herrings of them all, said Elie from Mov.

And soon salted and pickled, said Sidsel from Gudum.

When eating a herring, one must remember to break its spine, lest one's own be broken instead, said Dorte.

It's true, said Apelone, the spine of the herring must be broken.

Or else the witches will get you, said Christenze.

Enough of your witch-talk, said Elisabeth, and at that same moment the knife cut into her finger. She yelped, and immediately Maren took her hand and put the finger in her mouth. The blood of her frozen digit had no temperature and tasted of herring. Christenze considered the sight of Maren with Elisabeth's finger in her mouth. Someone, everyone, looked up, yet as one they continued to prepare the fish. Elisabeth snatched back her hand. She turned to Christenze.

Are you never going to marry? she said.

I think it is too late for me, said Christenze.

But aren't you lonely? said Elisabeth.

I have Maren and all of you, I hope, said Christenze.

You likely have the money to do as you want, being noble and all, said Else from Mov.

Christenze hasn't a shilling, said Maren.

Do you think I would sit here and gut herring with you, if I had money? said Christenze.

I hope by God that you would, said Maren.

God has nothing to do with it, said Dorte.

Is it true that you've got no money? Sidsel from Gudum said. I thought all the nobles had money.

Sometimes when I come home late from a gathering I am so tired, said Elisabeth, that I forget to say my prayers before going to bed. Then I am pricked with sin and become so terribly afraid that I won't meet any of you in Paradise.

They fell silent. Karen scratched at my wax; some of me came away under her fingernails and was gone the moment she jumped down from the bench.

We are all of us afraid of not meeting in Paradise, said Maren.

Does that mean that you won't be coming to the Lucia fest?

None of us will meet in Paradise, it was Apelone who spoke. Dorte laughed. The women had stopped cleaning the herring.

What are you saying? said Elisabeth.

You know what I mean, Apelone replied.

No, I won't be coming to the Lucia fest.

Elisabeth rose. At the edge of their circle she paused, and to my great surprise turned to me, the wax child:

How lucky you are, little thing, that you will go to neither Heaven nor Hell.

There was a faraway look in her eyes. I should rather have been a doll.

Then, before leaving, she turned towards Karen and said, Never marry a priest.

They said that hundreds of years ago, the herring in their time of frolic amassed in shoals as dense and as deep as the fjord itself, and could be scooped then into the boats with the bare hands. Or that one could thrust one's sword into the strait and spear three or four at a time. And still now it was the great wonder of Aalborg, it was the time of the herring monopoly, and to fish the herring was as if to pull money from the sea to those who were skilled in the craft.

When they had finished preparing the herring, they then became packing wives who packed the fish into barrels. They became salting wives; they became herring queens. And the scales of the fish were everywhere, like snow or ashes in their hair.

And I was in the king's ear, and I was in the king's mouth, and I was in the king's loose tooth and in the quicksilver of his liver, and did hear. A scratching of the pen across the paper as he wrote a royal letter to his deputy, Otto Skeel, king's lieutenant of Dueholm Monastery in the vicinity of Aalborg: Know, that since it has come to our ear that in our district of Aalborghus is said to be a noblewoman, Jomfru Christenze Axelsdatter Kruckow by name, who is reputed to be a witch, and that since it has been presented to us that there be a pastor, Magister David Klyne by name, who will seek to charge the jomfru of witchcraft, we thus command you and wish that you to the best of your ability endeavour discreetly to gather convincing evidence about the aforesaid jomfru, and that the same pastor do as he see fit by the power vested in him.

Someone said, I need a break. I need a success. My child bites at the nipple. You must wean him, I tell you. I need a lover, or a spirit that might give me more in my pocket to spend on frivolous things. You could have both, I could help you. It helped when I began to think of Lars as one of the children. Laughter. You must let them go aside to vent, then they will come back when they are good again. But can you sleep with him when you think like that? I spread my legs and hold my nose. Laughter. Do you not miss having someone in whom to confide? Only unmarried girls talk like that! You are all my confidantes. I do not think it bad, it could be much worse. Indeed, it could. Certainly, it could. We all know how it could be. All of us do. We know. How it could be. Yes, how it is for some. Yes, how it is for one in particular. How do you think she is feeling? Have you spoken to her? I have not spoken to her in a long time. I am worried about her. Yes, I am too. How are you feeling?

Someone in the hall says, I've heard she can steal folk's good fortune. My mistress hears them through the door. Christenze is surely not a witch. A bead of sweat clings to her temple. Inside her room the afternoon is illuminated like hollowed glass. The air is filled with the cries of traders and gulls. Outside, the air belongs to the fjord, the air is dense with moisture, milky violet where edged against the buildings. She struggles to breathe. It is as if with every inhalation she is poisoned by that which is Aalborg. Here at the table her palms appear strange, like two breasts, or as if she held in each a custardy pudding, and down in the street she sees Peder Fisker come by, there is a man at his side, they halt, and Peder gesticulates towards the house; the other man, at first unfamiliar to her, looks up, his face a disc at the bottom of the street, and Christenze recognizes him, it is Anne Bille's brother, his mouth opens, a small darkness, and he says something to Peder, but she cannot hear what. She cannot move. She is almost wax. Her hands are too heavy for her to lift. The elegant, audacious devices by which she normally manoeuvres desert her. She cannot remember which way she goes, this rather dishevelled figure in a petticoat bearing Anne Bille's initials. A draught slithers from the window and to walk the staircase is as if to step upon a mirror. She has been utterly alone in this world, and up to a certain point it has been a delight. But after Maren that form of freedom has been lost to her. She has become afraid. Christenze has not divulged to Maren what happened in Funen, about Anne and Ousse. Now the rumour has caught up with her and soon it will reach Maren and the others too.

In the garden behind the house, the red ticks gather like flames at the trunks of the lime trees. Beneath the drying sheets stands a basket of cherries. It is crocodile weather. It is the axe-age. It is the slightest waft of dry grass, and Christenze ties her boots. She is a white chrysanthemum in black leather. Her feeling is not good. She is losing her pace. She loves too many in Aalborg, and Aalborg is a lead weight on its way to the core of the Earth. They fall at speed. She cannot recognize the woman of whom they speak inside the house, though it is meant to be her. Footsteps approach, the mistress of the house.

There is someone wishing to speak to you.

Who is it?

It is Otto Skeel.

The king's lieutenant?

What have you done, Christenze?

I have done nothing.

You promised you would do it no more, not after Nakkebølle, if only you could live with me.

I have done neither more nor less than all others have done.

And I was in the king's ear, and I was in the king's mouth, and I was in the king's loose tooth and in the quicksilver of his liver, and did hear a rip of paper as he tore open the letter and read what Otto Skeel had written: It has been told to us that a man and a girl in Aalborg will witness and confess that they have seen and heard Jomfru Christenze Axelsdatter Kruckow inside the house of one known in the town to be a witch by the name of Maren Kneppis. Here she is believed with others to have employed sorcery and magic. Outside the mayor Niels Iversen's house one morning were found broken pots containing piss and excrement, and in the garden of mayor Frederik Christensen had been set snares and yarn, and afterwards this Frederik Christensen has deceased at an age of seventy-two years. In conversations with folk in Aalborg and environs, Jomfru Christenze Axelsdatter Kruckow has on numerous occasions been exposed and denounced to have committed many misdeeds and to have practised the most malevolent witchcraft, for instance to have cast a spell upon the wife of the magister David Klyne, pastor at the Church of Our Lady, thereby to have deprived her of her wits and senses. Moreover, a servant girl of Sæby in the employment of the merchant Christen Stubdrup of Aalborg became ill at the time of St John's Day after encountering Jomfru Christenze Axelsdatter Kruckow and her society and delaying them in their gathering. The jomfru's coven further includes Apelone Ibsdatter, who is the woman of a goldsmith and is well known by the town's king's lieutenants and mayors for controversies and cases concerning theft, though none has led to sentence. It is the belief of the aforementioned pastor that besides Jomfru Christenze Axelsdatter Kruckow, Maren Kneppis and Apelone Ibsdatter charges should also be brought against Dorte Kjærulf, since it is claimed that like the other three she did threaten and denounce his wife. Another witness has told that at the hour of around ten of evening in June while standing in an attic chamber he did happen to look out of the window when a number of swine came along the church path and did enter the church, and that subsequently he heard someone sermonizing from within or baptizing an infant, and that when the baptism was done he saw a person leave the church, whereafter the swine emerged one by one and set themselves in a row, and that there came several cats bounding along the path and did set themselves likewise, one cat between each swine, and the swine and the cats did speak to each other as if they were human.

Cast some blood of a hare into the fire, so that it makes a smell, then all the girls of the house will piss themselves. Or give them blood from a bat and those who have mixed with men will piss themselves.

God, I'm sick of her, says Apelone in the church, and I know it because Maren has taken me with her, hidden in the pit of her arm. Apelone has been demoted to a row at the rear, but could not care less. Dorte too has been sent to the back, though is furious. Now Dorte is seated further from the altar than her own portrait in the painting her family has donated to the church. It is Elisabeth's Klyne who has moved them. Apelone tears corners from the hymn book during the singing and rolls them into tiny pellets to throw at Elisabeth.

What have you heard about her?

I have heard everything about her.

Tell me.

She is quite altered and has begun to do penitence.

What do you mean?

She has become a good, Christian woman.

Oh no, the worst.

I know. She has told Klyne all sorts of stories about us.

Like what?

About how much she has sacrificed and that she is very devout, while we are very wicked.

And she is as pure as snow?

Exactly.

And has it changed the good priest?

What do you think?

As they file out after the service, the slit of Maren's ice-green dress sleeve parts and my eyes can peep out. Maren has taken Christenze by the hand, Dorte laughs out loud at something Apelone has said. But Christenze halts and the others sense immediately that something is not right, they follow her gaze and there stands the king's lieutenant Otto Skeel with his silver-bound cane. With him are Anne Bille's brother and another, dour-faced man without hair.

Who is the bald one?

That is Hideous Høeg.

Why is he looking at us?

He is the king's lieutenant's own executioner.

And what does he want with us?

Have you not heard the rumour about Christenze? It is Apelone who speaks.

There is a rumour of witchcraft about me, my mistress says.

All the way from Funen, says Apelone, from what I hear.

I am not afraid of them, says Dorte, and wrinkles her nose, an aged child puffing herself up. Maren kisses Christenze fleetingly on the cheek. Paradise must wait, she says.

They laugh. But in their laughter is disquiet, and they go home separately. Along the way, through the slit of Maren's sleeve, I observe four rats, a fallen quince-apple, a wooden beaker now split, one thousand two hundred raindrops that strike the stone.

There were only two. They met at the gutter between their houses.

Elisabeth, how are you? We have not seen each other in some time, said one.

Thank you, Christenze, I am well, said the other, as long as God wishes.

And the children, are they well too?

Yes.

And Klyne?

He is fine.

Won't you come with us to the Lucia fest, Elisabeth?

It is dangerous for me to associate with you.

Dangerous? In what way?

I forget to pray whenever we have been together.

Surely that is not dangerous?

To me it is.

Why?

Because my soul is weak.

Says who?

I think in fact I have always sensed it. That there is something wrong with me.

Did Klyne put this in your head?

I am fortunate to have a husband who is so understanding.

If there is something wrong with you, Elisabeth, then what of me? I must be an impossible case.

I have thought so myself.

You have?

I have been concerned about you.

You have been concerned about me? Does he still hit you?

That is unchristian talk, Christenze.

Unchristian? Is that what the two of you call me in your house?

You cannot escape the rumour.

Which is what?

A pause follows in which I hear nothing other than the gulls, a distant clash of steel and anvil, and I taste grains of light, iron. How, with my false mouth? Gutless, nerveless, and yet: taste. She repeats her question, and an answer is then forthcoming:

That you are . . . that you have performed acts of witchcraft.

And you believe that?

I don't know what it is that we do when we are at Maren's house.

Tell me, Elisabeth, is it witchcraft, when we are at Maren's house?

I think perhaps it is.

But surely you are not so stupid?

It is you who is the stupid one. To think you cannot see that Satan himself has tempted you.

I see quite clearly, my dear Elisabeth. And to share such notions with Klyne may have repercussions.

I am not afraid.

You should be. You should be terrified.

Are you threatening me?

I am trying to protect you!

I do not want your protection! Feh. Witch-hag!

Get to hell, Elisabeth! And do not come running to me the next time Klyne is after you.

Elisabeth resorts to a familiar, feeble voice:

How can you do this to me, well knowing that my soul is weak? How can you heap such anger on me? I do not think it good for us to associate.

Elisabeth, I didn't mean—

I must go.

Will you come to the Lucia fest?

But there is only the patter of rain and the two women who hesitate.

I am a child shaped in beeswax. I live with my mistress. From my place in the ground I observe the humans, their comings and goings. Two houses further along the street lives Elisabeth with the watery eyes. Colourless eyes almost, in which I bathe. Inside Elisabeth an unquelled suspicion resides. Something within her that unlike the rest cannot become soil. A rusty spade. A rusty droplet. A pair of feet made of rusted scrap. A sun of horn, and a brass spoon in Elisabeth's hand as she watches the hens in the run, and their eyes, full of sand, are like berry-black mirrors: the shiny, staring eyes of the hens dart like stars and mingle with the grain she scatters for them. Elisabeth, she is as the rain that shatters itself like glass upon the street. October wanes. It is early morning. The dewy grass wets the hem of her dress. Behind her, in the house, the servant girl is lighting the fire in the grate. At a certain time of the morning everything is dangerous. Before one is brought into use. Three strikes of the church clock wash by her. Her previous life, before she was married to Klyne, seems to her like a distant journey. The days revolve in the same way, the ritual begins, Klyne sermonizes in the church, and then soon it is the darkened afternoon with its furry edges and the servant girl will pour her a glass of claret that she will sip as Klyne talks, and she will float away upon her thoughts there in the vivid and velvety sitting room in which she is encased, and will sense again how she slides downwards into the earth underneath the house, to the remnants of bone and detached teeth that are settled there, and how, namelessly she becomes a part of a fertile soil. Elisabeth stands now stock-still in the garden. She allows it all to laugh at her. She looks up towards the sky and sees strings and black yarn draped among the trees. Someone, or something, must have done this under cover of the night. Their cat's cradle of looping figures winds this way and that, as if the trees were a web deposited by some passing god of chaos. A feeling of falling backwards, though she is already on her seat in the grass, soaked increasingly by the drizzle, beslimed by the eggs she was gathering only moments ago. She had not noticed them break. The path back to the house is long, endless. Elisabeth walks upon the surface of the darkness. But darkness is a membrane. And inside the membrane she can see a large egg. Around the egg is a red, pulsating aura. And from underneath the egg come powerful sparks of light. The strings in the trees sway wetly back and forth. Elisabeth looks down and discovers her arm to be composed of tiny incandescent grains. The taste in her mouth is of wickerwork, rain and butter. For a prolonged moment she is a doll. For a prolonged moment in the grass she is me.

She had been feeling for a time that something bad was about to happen. One day when Apelone went down to the fjord to see if the ships were on their way back, she looked at the steel-grey waves and realized that all her words were gone from her. The list in her mind that outlined the order of her day was vanished, and faces too. At once she was naked to the world, standing at the fjord and unable to remember what she had intended to do there. And there was a wind too that went through bone and marrow, as if she was a lock of hair and the wind a comb. Three old women approached then from the sea, they came unhurried over the waters and their figures were hunched and bent. Their wet hair clung to their faces. These were the herring queens, Aalborg's underwater deities. Apelone knew where the unlocked doors were, she had learned to steal without being discovered. On the few occasions she and Anders had been dragged before the court for the pettiest matters, she had found no difficulty in talking their way out. But something was changed and she felt unease. Last year at Bradsted they had burned a weaver woman, and now they had come for Mette, the cunning woman from Ulsted. In March, a number of men rode to Ulsted to sit upon her jury. At Vadum they came for Ane Lumpens. The herring queens knew all there was to know about the fjord and its cold waters, about the fish and the sandy bed, the gentle-eyed treasure of the mussel. Apelone understood now that the herring queens were an ill omen. She imitated their movements as she returned to the house, and continued the tale she told of herself. Apelone would do anything to avoid poverty. She knew every trick in Aalborg, knew that everything and everyone had a price, and knew its amount. Apelone knew that a person can never know enough, that one should always be ready, never regret an action that brought you closer to safety and shelter. She tied up her hair, called upon her girls, and began.

Each morning, Maren saw another leaf fall from the tree outside her window. Each morning, another chapter and the children's hungry heads. She heard inside herself little clicks, as though of metal. Night dripped down her back, a silvery hydrant emptying itself of her nocturnal person. The day belonged to the children. She saw herself in the polished stone and saw her mother's face. The middlemost day in November opens itself like a bottomless, felted scabbard. Rold Forest's heart thuds against the downy walls. Maren is unaware that in a few weeks' time, when the king's lieutenants come for her, she will feel such a violent stab in her breast when they take her away, nor that she will look back then at the children and the farmstead, at all this toil that has worn her into the ground; she does not know that when they come for her and she turns and looks back at the house, at her children who are standing open-mouthed and unspeaking, that when then she tries to smile, and the magpie as so many times before takes to the wing from the tree behind the house, that at that moment, when from those lieutenants' clutches she sees her home for the first time as a whole, as if only then it has become visible to her, that as they remove her from it, she will feel such a violent stab in her breast that she thinks she will die from it.

I heard it said that a woman should be loyal to one man. Her husband, her father, or God. I saw the shadows of night unfold their tendrilly roots into the soil. I concealed treasures, I gathered stores for the winter. No wax children were made any more. A thing of glass was my liver. Cold rain ran over my pate like a sleet wig. Otto Skeel, a king's lieutenant, sat in his monastery at Dueholm. Manderup Parsberg, a king's lieutenant, sat in his castle in Aalborg. Anders Friis, a king's lieutenant, sat in his manor house at Sejlstrup. They consulted their books of demonology, and there read: The woman is more easily tempted by Satan, for she is weaker than the man in both body and soul. And they read: The woman is a wicked and imperfect animal. When a woman weeps she weaves snares, and labours to deceive a man. And they read: When a woman thinks alone, she thinks evil. She is not capable of good thoughts. And they read: The woman is feebler than the man and more easily charmed by the Devil. And they read: The word woman is another expression for desires of the flesh. And they read: All witchcraft stems from fleshly desires, which in the woman are insatiable. And they read: At times the man may be deprived of his virile member. When the member is in no way stirred, this is a sign of frigidity of nature; but when it is stirred and becomes erect, but yet cannot perform, it is a sign of witchcraft. And they read: Women are more credulous, by nature's hand more ready to receive the influence of a disembodied spirit. They have slippery tongues and are unable to conceal from their fellow women those things which they know through their evil arts. Since they are weak they find a secret and easy manner of vindicating themselves by witchcraft. And they read: In this dusk of the world, when sin is flourishing on every side and in every place, when charity is growing cold, the evil of witches and their iniquities superabound. And they read: Where there are many women, there are many witches.

In Aalborg, the needle of St Botolph's spire pierces the tongue of the sky. The wind moves over tracts of land to which no one yet lays claim. One by one, the decades pass over me like the wind upon the fjord. And yet I would cry if only I had eyes that could cry. In the early morning, before Maren and the others are to be taken by the lieutenant and thrown into the dungeons for their sorcery, I will go to the oak grove where boulders left by the retreating ice lie, secluded like sanctums among the trees. Give me, for the place of sacrifice, a twig of azalea burning. I hold no sympathy for upright things, buildings and laws. Humankind is a fool. I pity my mistress. Deep under Aalborg is a red and terrible altar, dark as a womb's interior. No one can escape it. Hatred comes to the one who trembles. I pity them, I pity my mistress, I pity Maren, and Maren's servant girl, I pity the humans, reckless, quickly absorbed and used up like nylon stockings that run the same evening they are worn. The humans are mouths which are opened far too often and run dry too quickly. Hundreds of years I have lain here and heard you chatter; you humans like so much to talk, from the moment you are born until you die you are engaged in babble. All that is around us will someday fall. Some of it sooner than you think. Christenze and Maren and Apelone and the others too will be forgotten. But not me. I shall be their idiot bell, and ring for no one in the dry soil. No wax child is merely a doll. Any wax child contains human parts. Now, bigger and bigger slabs of coast detach into the sea. Soon the waves will wash over the peninsula. All those who lived in Aalborg then are now dead and in their houses live new people who resemble them. With each death I shrank. Do not ask for whom I speak. Do not ask on whose behalf. I speak for you.

Now Peder Fisker cuts through the Latin Alley alongside the hospital wall, moonlight skims the piss-wet cobbles. The hospital lies quiet in the darkness, Aalborg lies quiet between the Kattegat and the Jammerbugt, and Peder has been out many hours in his boat. He is filled with the coldness of the sea, the inky-mouthed sea of night. His legs are restless and he must walk it off; he lights his pipe. It is the night of St Lucia and he is in search of a place to drink. There is barely a light in any window. Only the moon and his stiffened fingers, a dryness to his eyes, a strange, wordless absence.

Take the water from the eye of a stallion that has not yet been led to a mare, and with it wet your own eyes, then all can be seen that would otherwise be unseeable, and this three mornings in succession.

I was a child shaped in beeswax. I was made like a doll the size of a human forearm. They had given me hair and fingernail parings from the persons who were to suffer. And again I was carried, this time by Maren, for many weeks under her clothing, and I was like a proper child, and my wax was softened by her warmth, but I was missing my first mistress. When the evening came and the carrying period was passed, something began to tremble in me, like a bluebell in the wind upon a cliff. It was the night of St Lucia, the twelfth of December, and the year was 1620. In Maren's sleeping room, all were gathered.

There was Christenze and Maren. There was Dorte and Apelone. There was Mette, and someone called Elle, and Maren Pedersdatter and Margrethe Hjulmands, and the wife of Gunder Vognkarl, and there was Christen Knudsen's woman and an old wife from Vorde whose name was Ane or Maren, and a Mette from Klarup, Else from Mov, Bodil and Sidsel from Gudum.

Maren entered with a candle in her hand and lay down upon the floor as if to give birth, and the others drew me out from under her skirts like I was a human child. And everyone laughed and sang and fell about each other, and Maren looked up at Christenze with that light in her eyes and Christenze had to kiss her.

It is true that someone was meant to be stricken, that someone was meant to suffer. These fingernail parts, these strands of hair Maren had meticulously pressed into my wax foot. But first and foremost they wished to commit to each other, first and foremost they wished to seal their association, to summon the golden servant, and now it was here, I took its place, and the women's hearts were up in their mouths, all of them opened their mouths and looked agitatedly around at each other, and in every mouth was seen a lustrous fleshy heart, and every one did fill the room with its drumming; even I, who have no heart, felt as if my own was in my mouth, and I cannot describe the sense of joy it gave me, and the moment stretched into infinity, time dissolved inside their circle, they took each other by the hand and began slowly to dance around me with their open heart-mouths. One after another they approached and spat into my face, and each then did swallow her heart, which slithered back into its proper place and was changed by the experience. And when Christenze's spit fell on my brow I nearly burst with arousal. The candles flickered and made it look like they were dancing upon a bonfire of shadows. They had initiated me with their spit, and they called me Elisabeth, for the fingernails and hair they had given into my foot besides their own were hers, I felt it immediately. But before they were able to complete the initiation, a banging was heard upon the windowpane and outside in the darkness a terrible face appeared.

It's Peder! Apelone cried.

Yes, in all damnation it is! he screeched back. Maren, you hag, so it's true, that you gad about for the sake of mischief!

His gaze went from one to another, and again he screeched into the wind, Do you think I'm stupid? When you are so many women together, it can only be in devilish pursuits! Even an idiot knows. I'll run now and tell the bailiff and the mayor.

His figure vanished. A distant light reflected in the black water of the fjord. They all stood transfixed and stared at each other. Then hell broke loose, and with much screaming and shouting they gathered their things and ran out of the house as fast as their feet could carry them. Maren snatched me up and set fire to my foot, the one in which the fingernails of the pastor David Klyne's wife were pressed, and I felt nothing other than a tension subside. Only the girl. Karen, remained after all others but her mother had fled, and she had seen it all.

Come here to me, sweetheart, Maren said, and the girl climbed on to Maren's lap, and there the woman sat and rocked her child and tried to stem the tears that were rolling down her face. She tipped back her head and opened her mouth in a silent scream. I saw the heart in her mouth once more. And the aorta spoke to me, signs as chains of gold in the night. With an arc of her foot Maren swept me underneath the bed.

Mother, ask me what a laceband is, said the girl.
What is a laceband?
It is a kind of ribbon by which to tie one's shirt.
That's right. Now it's time to sleep.

On the night of St Lucia, when everyone has said the evening prayer, the girls are to say: *Lucia the White will show me tonight whose cloth I shall spread, whose bed I shall make, whose child I shall bear, whose true love I shall be, in whose arms I shall sleep.* Whereupon the true love will appear in the room and there will be light where they are.

A WITCH TRIAL

Were I not a wax child, I think I could have been a wound. But preferably I would be a root vegetable in warm soil, a wild carrot or an onion without eyes. Why should a wax child be kept alive when it lives by itself, without human interference, when first it has been made? Why should a book be kept wet and sodden? Why should the sheep, the lamb and the he-goat be driven across the mud? The wind turns the pages of the book with the sound of a cart fitfully drawn over cobbles. By strength of Aalborg's colours and smells, I might almost become a daisy of blood. No one listened to me. They hung the linen to be bleached. I had lost my power, my illicitness now finally confirmed, and the rumour travelled. One night someone tried to draw a ring of salt around the castle of Aalborghus, but when morning arrived nothing had happened. The magic failed. From inside the king's lieutenant's chambers issued soon a ceaseless flow of words. And numerous letters were dispatched with haste. And ledgers were begun. And someone drew up a map. And someone updated a list. And someone priced a sprig as yet without bud. And if that daisy of blood dissolved into a fabric of woven moiré that was like a flamy surface of bark, a child's dark eyes upon me, and the hen soaked with blood, headless. Someone's saying the same prayer over and over. I am a dull knife.

And I was in the king's ear, and I was in the king's mouth, I was in his breath, I was in the gold ring on his finger, in its still-remaining recollection of being water, in the bone of his buttons, in the horn of his buckles, in the mother-of-pearl of his cufflinks; I was in the coating of his tongue, I was everywhere in the king, like a dream or a poisoning, in the threaded gauze of his bandage, in his chuckles of joy and in his rage, in the kind envelopment of fat around his organs, in the kingly frame, in the kingly body, like the smallest music, fluid was I, as the sperm cell in his blood was I, the frogly black bairn was I, the wax child, without vocal cords I cried, smooth and accursed I slipped into the letter he sealed and sent on its way; in his words, and in the grains of sand he strewed casually like dots of vanilla across the ink in order that it might dry, and I was there as he folded the paper, there, as small as a speck in the eye, in the words as they travelled towards Aalborg, as they arrived in the hand of Otto Skeel, and in Otto Skeel's eyes I was reflected, and flew up, flew out, flew away, with the words of the king, these words written: Know, that it has come to our ear that Jomfru Christenze Axelsdatter Kruckow, residing in our borough of Aalborg, both previously and now again has been denounced for witchcraft and for this reason it is our will that she at once be arrested and subjected to your rigorous examination. Furthermore, it is our will that you, Otto Skeel, ensure her secure confinement and allow not that she be left unattended. Likewise, it is our will that you detain the other women of Aalborg so denounced, and with them proceed.

Now it comes to me in a vision – a blazing field of red mirrors advancing from the sea towards the coast, the rain shower's dale. A mussel's shell with a human skull for its pearl. My wax mouth cannot be opened. I must push myself to the furthest limit and find pleasure there. My Christenze, now led to the tax office at Aalborghus. There sits heavily on his chair the king's lieutenant Manderup Parsberg, a good-natured man of years, there stand Otto Skeel and Anders Friis, the two younger king's lieutenants, there stands Hideous Høeg, executioner of Aalborg; Christenze knows them all, has been here before in this brown room with its elaborately carved panelling on ceiling and walls, whose smell is like the inside of a letter. There is Christenze, there is Maren, there is Dorte, and Apelone. Detained and charged they stand. In front of them, as if to form a looking-glass image, the four men are engaged in discussion, and the women are as if invisible to them. There is some disagreement as to where the accused are at first to be held. Outside, it is afternoon, dark, December. There is something out there in the wind, only Christenze is aware of it, something wanting to get inside to where they stand, a wolf or an elf-creature, perhaps. Now she sees the two stones that hung like eyes in the air before her that time at Nakkebølle. The stones dither in their suspension, to the right of Otto Skeel's face, and it is as if Anne Bille is now standing behind Christenze and is blowing into her ear. A small part of Christenze, though no more perhaps than a pill-box of her blood and gristle, or a single finger-bone, a toe, still belongs to Anne. Christenze will not acknowledge it. The fact that certain ties can never be broken. That there remains in her a strangely fleecy mist, a desire for Anne still. A desire that Christenze, when she closes her eyes in the company of Anne, in Anne's arms, with the inside of her eyes may taste Anne's spit. Or that Christenze's eye may be a tongue, and the inside of her eyelid a sliver of Anne's wetness, such that Christenze, in blinking, may taste Anne. My mistress's thoughts drift away, as if already she has given up, as if she could detach herself from what is occurring in the brown office room. Can we lock up Christenze Kruckow with the other three? is what the voices are discussing. The eye-stones drop to the floor with the clatter of weapons; a dog darts forward and licks them. Yes, there is no hindrance, the voices conclude. Are we certain it is witchcraft they have performed? they say. That is for the court to decide, they say. The examination will tell us, they say. What other reasons than witchcraft do you consider possible? they say. Superstition, dullness of mind, melancholy, thick blood, they say. What did it cost to burn the cunning girl from Ulsted? they say. I have the expenses recorded in the ledger somewhere, they say. Do you think it will come to that? Apelone's nosebleed coagulates and has begun to itch. Dorte has difficulty seeing through her swollen eye. Maren is missing a tooth. Christenze's head is swimming still after the blow. None of them speaks. None of them can form a thought to be uttered. Not one among the eight who are present in the room fully comprehends what they are allowing out of its lair. And I, I am a wax child, secreted from the scaly glands of the honeybee's abdomen, of rose hip, propolis, pollen, dread, quince, longing, yeast dough, age, and ever young, with infinity's secret in my folds. They consult their ledger; they read aloud from it: Ale for the executioner, two nights: 2 marks. Reasonable, by any account, they say. Wait, there is more, they say: For five barrels of tar: 5 marks. A ladder for the girl: 20 shillings. For the executioner for putting her to her death: 9 daler. Payment to a man for assisting in her night-time capture: 4 daler, they say. No paltry sum, they say. Indeed, a handsome payment, they say, and continue. For the witnesses called to the hundred court: 5 marks. A pair of shoes for her, since she was barefoot when taken into custody: 3 marks, they say. Indeed, they say. Indeed, and again they continue: For the summons: 4 shillings. For the judgement of the provincial court: 6 marks. And then there was the boy clerk, a half-mark, the judgement of the hundred court, half a daler, bed and board for the provincial court, two nights, likewise half a daler, they say. And then too the cost of her detention, including payment for the ones who attended her those two nights, they say. That came to 3 marks, they say. And further: Has an amount been included for those who conducted the examination? To which they say, Not as far as can be seen. A mussel is alive as long as it is closed; this is the thought in Apelone's head. I don't think we should view it as a series of expenses, they say. Rather it should be considered as a series of undertakings, a service carried out for public good, they say. In any circumstance we have no choice, the court shall proceed and take its course, they say. Witchcraft is a very grave business, they say, and look askance at the waiting women who stand as yet with hands bound. Let me, Apelone thinks, let me be a stake, frayed by saltwater, around which mussels congregate and thrive. The costs can be covered without difficulty, they say. I don't think we should view it as a series of expenses, they say. Cleansing cannot be calculated in money, they say. And the thought in Apelone's head is that she will drown herself in the fjord, directly outside the window, as soon as they are released, that she will give herself to the herring queens and reside with them. Let us wait and see whether they will be acquitted, they say. I doubt it, they say. It is the very reason we have a secular court, they say. Will you make sure to call in the witnesses? they say. It must cost what it costs, they say. Has clay the ability to fly? Christenze wonders. Has wax? Where is my child now? Is mud able to breathe or raise itself above itself? I need to be canny, Christenze thinks, but she is inside a pod, and the pod is lined with a whitish lint; she is the smallest mouth, without body, in the belly of the pod, where purple lips tremble with the smallest teeth. What are we doing? she wonders. I sound a tone that renders all else meaningless, she thinks, and every noise perplexes, and everyone else is so far from me, she thinks, I strive to listen, she thinks, now they lay their heavy hands upon my shoulders, now they lead us from the room in single file. Are we going home now? No, we are to descend a narrow stair? Why do we not resist? God loves us. I do not think they can put a spell on us, someone says. Clearly it is not correct, someone says. That is obviously incorrect, someone says. Who cares? someone says. Everyone does, someone says. Come, sit down, shuffle closer, someone says, I'm cold. Come, let me warm you, someone says. I didn't know we'd be here so long, someone says, or else I'd have put on warmer clothes. What day is it? someone says. It is the fifteenth. We near the bottom of the funnel, someone says. Come, let me relieve your pain, someone says. Does it hurt where he struck you? One takes the other's arm and rubs it with both her hands, the wrist and forearm. One says, Now by my words the pain will shrink. Now by my nine words the pain will shrink as my words do likewise. From nine to eight, from eight to seven, from seven to six, from six to five; now by my words the pain will shrink, from five to four, from four to three, from three to two, now the pain will shrink, from two to one, from one to nothing.

Someone in the casemates said, Your hand in the darkness is very soft. Someone in the casemates said, We are alive. As yet we are alive. Someone in the casemates said, Will you make yourself invisible? We are alive, someone said. I cannot see, someone said. We are alive. Something smells burnt, someone said. I cannot see. Is something burning? someone said. We are alive. I cannot see, someone said. Here, take my hand. The main thing is that we are alive. As yet we are alive. Who is it who speaks? someone said. It is only me, someone said. Who is that? It is us. Apelone. Is this your hand? someone said. No, it is mine. Is it you? I cannot see. I cannot either. Something is burning, someone said. Are we all here? Yes. Come over to the keyhole, so the light can fall upon your face. Yes, I will, someone said. Why is your skin so waxy and pale? Why do your eyes stare so? All the better to see you. Something is among us. What something? Something that is not us, someone said. What do you mean? I cannot see, someone said. The main thing is that we are alive. As yet we are alive. Yes. Hello? someone said. Is anybody there? someone said. Maren, are you there? Maren? Where is Maren? someone said. Something smells burnt, someone said. I cannot see, someone said. Quiet. I hear something, someone said. Keys that rattle, someone said. Now they are coming.

Someone in the darkness of the casemates said, We're alive. As yet we're alive. We is us. It's Maren. It's Apelone. It's Dorte, and Christenze. You had a strange little wax child. We were meant to perform magic with it. You had such beautiful eyes. You always became wet so quickly. We are in the casemates, in the dungeon of Aalborghus. We talk to each other all day long. From our four corners. We have nothing else to do. You had with you a loaf of rye bread you would not share. You silly woman, Apelone. Is that loaf hard and dry now? Someone in the darkness of the casemates said, The worst one is Otto Skeel. He always grabs a squeeze whenever they come in to see to us. And he talks boastfully of how he knows the king. And he says they soon will question us one by one. People are so obsessed with our death. Someone kneeled and through the peephole in the door observed tired glossy images of the world.

It is the darkest of times, December. From the curvature of the Earth, minutes run like droplets from the day. Aalborg extends its sleep, people go drowsily about in the dusk. Merchants cannot believe that light will return. Heavily pregnant women cannot believe they will give birth. It is the winter solstice. In the dripping dawn, the fox sneaks by their cell with blood about its chops: in its eyes glow the chemicals of morning. They set them to peel asparagus, said I, the wax child. The object that could speak.

It was two or three in the afternoon when Peder Fisker came walking along Slotsgade and cut across in front of Aalborghus. The executioner had got hold of Apelone and was tormenting her there. Otto and Hideous Høeg were wanting to know who had cast a spell on Mayor Frederik Christensen, and if she knew of witches in Aalborg. And Peder heard Apelone reply that she knew nothing of it. Whereupon Otto instructed Hideous Høeg to tighten the leg-screw yet further. And then Apelone screamed and implored them to say which of them they wanted her to denounce. And then Peder heard Otto say that surely she knew best herself. And then she gave them the name of Klyne's woman, Elisabeth. And then Otto replied that this was a lie and had no truth to it. And then there was a whispering, a murmur of voices, but what was said Peder could not hear. And then Apelone cried, No, not Dorte! And then laughter rang out across the courtyard, and then Otto's voice instructed the hideous one to tighten the leg-screw yet further, for no doubt she would recuperate. And Apelone screamed again and implored them for the sake of God to release her, and then her voice calmed and became almost serene, Peder thought. And then the voice said: I am the witch. The voice said: And Maren too. The voice said: Release me and go with me into the church, and I'll tell you everything you want to know.

A shadow passed by in the crack of light underneath the door. Karen, is it you? someone asked. Yes, said the girl, and I have brought wood avens, it will help. And through the crack she slipped them the straggly plant. One after another they partook of it, then handed it on to the next. And when the plant came to the one among them who had returned from the examination, she began to laugh in such a way that her eyes watered, and she held out her hand and said, Look how black that glove! What is it? asked the girl from the other side of the door. Nothing, someone said in reply. There is nothing I can do, said the one who had returned from the examination, I could fly from here, if I wished, she said. Then let us see, someone said. Maren did it, said the one who had returned from the examination, Christenze did it. She laughed, and added: I couldn't help it, they forced me, have mercy. And she belched then into the dimness, and after that came a cry, 'Tis Maren! 'Tis Maren who is the witch! And someone replied, Fret not, they've already fetched her. What? Who? Maren, someone said, she has already been fetched, it is already begun.

If you want not to feel anything during torture, write down these lines on a scrap of paper and then swallow it: *Dismas et Gestas damnatur potestas. Disma et Gestas damnatur. Ad astra levatur.* And when you are to be tortured, say then: *This rope is soothing to my limbs, as the Holy Virgin's milk is to our Lord.*

In this darkness, beneath a bank of earth, my mistress sat, and imperceptibly it came to her, like a creeping stiffness in the neck, the thought that she could save herself. The other women in the dungeon seemed increasingly to belong together, in their nature distinguished from her, with husbands and children and common tales of their youth. Could she, with some small measure of cunning, some small measure of fortune, extricate herself from them and their fate? A familiar loneliness had returned, as if Christenze until then had forgotten that she was made to be alone. There was a lightness, these wings in her that now must be tested again. It does not befit me to be a martyr, she thought. Where is my wax child? she asked. Karen has it, someone said. Christenze nodded, and sensed, like the gleaming-eyed hare, her escape route. Maren licked her finger and drew with her spit on the back of Christenze's hand. And the spit, absorbed then into my mistress's skin, told me much and at length of her quite ordinary blood and its quite ordinary and completely human paths, its unlit shafts, its flexing tubes, a heart.

And as the eye's membrane, an osmotic screen, a curtain of the oracles, I breathed. Light itself (that light which never will talk, the subterranean light) was refracted and transformed upon the membrane into secretion. And my mistress's eyes turned towards the horizon's clearing sky. The light descended and everything was struck by it, each and everyone stood beneath the stars, and were a single accord beneath the dome-shaped sphere of the heavens. Where was her fleetness? Why, in her cold corner, did she merely lie and watch as one by one they were taken away, and later brought back, watch as they grew more and more emaciated, hear an animal that cried like a newborn infant in the lateness of morning?

The forest reached from Aalborg, northwards towards Ugilt, its fringes no more than scrub, a thickening denseness of lingonberry and juniper. The low-slung oakwoods ran east as far as to the sea, clambering across the moor and shaping shelters underneath its crowns, where a comb of horn was pushed up from the ground with an inscription concerning head lice; where appeared a jug, as round as a cabbage, pearls enough to fill a hand, of Roman glass, and further south-east not far from Gjerrild, in the dolmen there, numerous precious metals, small parts, coins and fragments of jewellery, silver and bronze. Jutland – the land itself a wax child, filled with horn and hair, with human remains, human tools, flutes and whistles carved in bone, and the wind became audible unto itself as it passed through them. In the dungeon Dorte whistled too. They took turns to sit by the door, where outside air might waft the face and be breathed, and Dorte whistled in reply to the howl of the wind. She thought about a marzipan mouth that had lain among others on a dish at the grocer's store, and smacked her lips to recall it, then turned to the others and said, I will get out of here, I have a plan, my son-in-law will come to my rescue, I cannot imagine otherwise.

She rubbed her face.

Do you really think so? said Maren, who after an absence of some days had returned with a broken hand, having disclosed nothing.

Dorte turned to Christenze.

Surely you will not accept this either? she said.

You ought to have been more careful, my mistress replied. I can hardly comprehend that you allowed Peder Fisker to see us.

What do you mean, allowed him to see us? said Maren.

You should have closed the shutters, my mistress said. How could you have been so stupid? But it is my own fault for not having seen it come. After all, you are only . . . peasants.

Christenze, Maren said.

I should not be here by any right, my mistress said. Do you understand? We have had such pleasant times together, Maren, but I am noble.

There at last we have it, said Dorte. I told you, she's always felt herself better than us.

I *am* better than you, my mistress said.

We are all of us equal before God, said Apelone.

No, that is not in fact true, my mistress said, and you do not believe it either, Apelone. No, I believe . . . but Christenze's words then trailed away, as Apelone tried absently to reach the tip of her nose with her tongue.

Do we mean nothing to you? Maren asked.

You mean everything to me, all of you, Christenze replied, and I pray to God that he will let you live, each and every one of you. Soon they will realize their mistake in keeping me here. Soon a letter will come from the king and explain it to them. These are but preliminaries, and when I am released I will be able to help you . . .

And how will you do that? asked Dorte.

You are stuck here with us, said Maren.

Shall I teach you to fly? said Apelone. Do you wish to be invisible?

Tell us, how will you get us out? Dorte asked.

Can you not see? Maren said. We are doomed, all of us, including you.

It is already begun, said Dorte.

It is already finished, said Maren.

It is already a thing of great beauty, said Apelone.

I can't listen to this, said Christenze. Can you or anyone else honestly say that I have concerned myself with witchcraft?

You made a wax child, did you not? said Apelone.

And you gave sheep's milk to defenceless women, said Dorte.

And you made me love you, said Maren.

The key rattled in the lock, and now entered Hideous Høeg.

Make yourselves ready, he said. Maren Kneppis is to stand before the court and you are all to attend with her.

Are we to go to the castle? said Apelone. Are we to wear silken robes?

To hell with it, whispered Dorte to Christenze. What is the plan?

Give me a minute to think, said Christenze.

Christenze, what is the plan? asked Maren.

I'm thinking, can't you see? Wait.

To win a trial, say these words as you tie a knot: *I shall tie a knot so firm. I shall tie his tooth and tongue, his hand and foot, and innermost heart. I shall tie his tooth and tongue, his liver and lung. Yes, his speech and language too, and quite as firm as the Devil stands in Hell. My words shall grow like grass in rain. Sun and moons shall perish before my foe is proven right over me. I sow my words here on the meadow green. I wish him trouble and strife. He shall find them both and the same shall he know. In three men's name.*

It is the third of May, 1621, the hawthorn is blossomed, the alder buckthorn tree and the purging buckthorn tree are blossomed, and all the white trumpeting flowers cast their mouths towards the bay and are answered by it.

The walls of the tax office at Aalborghus Castle are clad with tapestries, and three windows give on to the fjord that drifts by, glittering as water does in its own deep time, a long arm that reaches into the land, and in the blood veins of the arm run the shoals of fish and shimmer each and every one in the sunshine of May month like rings meshed together in chain mail.

The castle is barely more than a two-storey, half-timbered manor, its buildings enclosing a courtyard, fortified by a dry moat beneath whose banked-up earth are the casemates.

Maren, Christenze, Dorte and Apelone stand now in the passage outside the tax office and wipe each other's faces with a cloth. How do I know all this? Because the fish told me. The blossom told me. The threads of the tapestries wailed and turned to whisper it.

In the tax office now a full thing-witness of eight good and upstanding men is assembled. And an ecclesiastical court comprising a bishop and three parish priests.

Now the four who are accused of witchcraft are fetched into the packed room. They recognize family members and neighbours. They are led into the dock. Maren sees that Karen is seated with her father, Olaf, and ceases then to listen to what is said concerning the charges brought against her. Instead, she sits and gazes upon Karen, whose face is half hidden underneath a bonnet. Her nose sticks out, and strands too of the fairest hair, known so well by Maren's palm, so quickly tousled it becomes at the nape. The girl has grown since December when they were imprisoned, and Maren thinks of the dress that belonged to one of the older girls, which she has kept for Karen to wear when she grows out of the old one, and perhaps there will be a chance before the court is adjourned to tell Olaf where it is kept. But now someone speaks her name.

Maren Kneppis, rise!

She rises. Karen is silent, far removed from her own face. She whispered to me in the night, but only when her girl-tears followed her words was I allowed to experience the wonder of weeping, for her tears fell upon my cheek as if they were mine.

When Otto Skeel showed Manderup Parsberg the letter he had received from the king concerning my mistress and told him of their correspondence, Manderup allowed Otto to take over, and Otto has been diligent in his preparations. Aided by Hideous Høeg, he has questioned the women in turn and gathered evidence, and he has ridden about and enquired of good and upstanding men as to what they might know, and with him he carries a number of written testimonies, and Apelone will be easy enough, she is already broken, Dorte will be more difficult, Christenze the most difficult of them all, but Maren, of whom many in Aalborg are fond, Maren, with her gentle heart and open character, Otto will question first, for if Maren breaks, the others will follow.

And how do I know this? I know, because the ink of Otto's pen told me, a droplet detached from the nib and splashed upon the planks of the floor, from where, through its toothless black mouth, it spoke.

As he reads out the charges against Maren, he looks upon the assembly and his tongue shapes his every word as if he was sucking a garlic-fried snail from its shell. He dwells upon a *linen cap*, Maren is accused of stealing a *linen cap*. He tells of Niels Iversen, the mayor who dropped dead after the women had pissed and shat outside his door in the night. He tells of the girl from Sæby who fell so gravely ill after delaying the women in their gathering. And he tells of swine and cats emerging from the church in the night. And now upon the benches there is much unease, and for this reason he moves on to speak about good fortune. For these women with their harmful magic have stolen the good fortunes of ordinary townsfolk and dealt them out among themselves. And many here today have surely felt their own good fortunes to have dwindled more quickly than before known, until eventually they had none. And he tells that twenty-two men of Hasseris and sixteen Aalborgers have testified concerning the rumour of witchcraft that has pursued Maren Kneppis through many years, and that it has been widely known that she understands how to perform the skills of witchcraft. And he asks Peder Fisker to take to the witness-stand and tell the court what he saw on the night of St Lucia. It annoys Otto that Maren keeps looking back over her shoulder. Is she not interested in what is going on? Is the woman indifferent to her fate? And then he realizes that she is looking at her youngest daughter.

The next witness I shall call is Karen Pedersdatter, Otto says.

And Karen is led to the stand, and Maren's head as if upon an axis swivels again that she may look at the girl.

What is your name? Otto asks.

Karen Pedersdatter.

And how do you know Maren Kneppis?

It is my mother's name.

Is it true that you saw your mother in the company of these women and a number of others on St Lucia night in December?

Yes, it is true.

Can you tell us what you saw?

Well, they were spitting and dancing, and my mother had a troll-child.

A troll-child? How did this occur?

She had it like you have a baby.

You mean she gave birth to it?

But now that I've said it, she will be coming home, won't she?

Can you tell me about the woman sitting over here?

That is Christenze, a friend of my mother's.

Are they good friends?

Sometimes she lies in my mother's bed. She lends my mother clothes. We play a game together on Thursdays, when I am in Christenze's house. I hide, and when she comes to look for me she says, Hide yourself well from the hangman!

You may return now to your father's side. Maren Kneppis, have you anything to say against this?

No, I have nothing to add, says Maren, and turns again so that when the girl passes by she may give her a beaming smile.

In the doorway of the tax office people squeeze together and crane their necks. A murmur rises as Klyne gets to his feet to take to the witness-stand.

These women, he says, his eyes upon the ones accused, harbour such jealousy towards me that they have cast illness upon my poor wife.

Klyne has much to say, and says it:

It all began when we took out a lamb to be slaughtered, he says, and when the slaughter took place our servant girl told us to remember to give some meat to Dorte Kjærulf, for she was a widow and prayed for us often. What do you mean, she prays for us? I asked the girl, who told me then that there were ceremonies they employed, Dorte and her cohorts, among whom were Apelone Guldsmeds, Christenze Kruckow and several others, and how the wives during these ceremonies writhed upon each other, and that they had a black snake among them, and that Dorte released the snake from a case when they were to pray, and that the serpent then crawled among them until they had prayed, and then they all waved their hands about and the snake slithered into its case again. My wife then asked if the girl could demonstrate to us in which manner they writhed upon each other, and the girl duly lay down on the floor to show us. It was at this instant the illness first struck my wife. She became quite white in the face and would not eat when evening came. In the night, I was awakened by her weeping very unpretentiously. I asked her what the reason was, but at first she would not say, only that she would bear the grief on her own, for I had much else to think about concerning my duties as a priest. However, I urged her to tell me, and the unfortunate woman could do no more to keep it in. She whimpered then so wretchedly and said she did not wish for anything bad to befall me, and I comforted her as best God gave to me the gift and beseeched her to pray every morning and evening to the Lord, and said that this would suffice to protect us. But she wept only more at this and insisted that as soon as any poor wretch forgot her prayers it was by nature the end of her, for devilish folk pursue with vigour those who forget to pray. Since that night she has never been satisfied and has moaned and wept so terribly and insisted that something bad soon will befall our house. She has always been a fearful person. But ever since she was stricken by this illness, so strange and peculiar that no physician has been able to explain it, but has called it unnatural . . . and it was so very clear to us that it was not until the girl told us about Dorte and the snake . . .

His words trail away. Christenze has now risen.

Can you or anyone else honestly say to me that I have concerned myself with witchcraft? she says. Or that any of these women at my side have concerned themselves likewise? That Maren Kneppis has? That which has been put forward here is no more than gossip and fabrication.

Christenze, a voice says behind her then. It is Elisabeth.

Christenze, let me. Elisabeth rises in the centre of the room. She goes towards the witness-stand. At the dock she halts. She smiles at them, a childish, secretive smile which they know from past times. She undoes a blue scarf from around her neck and presses it into Dorte's hand. And as Elisabeth then takes to the stand, the women in the dock are embraced by her familiar scent. Wine, rain, roses.

Tell us your name, Otto says.

Elisabeth David Klynes.

And you are married to the pastor David Klyne?

Yes.

You are not named as a witness in the case, Otto says.

I hope you will make an exception. I intend no malice. I am here only to say the truth.

Let her speak, someone shouts from the doorway.

Christenze smiles at Elisabeth. Elisabeth turns towards Otto.

I know a thing or two about these women, she says.

From the building's outermost rafter a droplet falls upon the back of a fire-bellied toad sitting still in the grass.

Let me tell you, she says, let me tell you, the worst that you think about them is true. At night in my dreams they have tortured and plagued me, and have seized upon and made fun of even the smallest error I have made, the slightest clumsiness.

Elisabeth's voice deepens:

I thank my husband that I left their society in time, before the Devil dug his claws into them. I thank God for allowing me back into his embrace that I might return to *father, mother and children*, the sanctity of family, instead of such a foul coven of women. They do nothing but slander and curse me.

In the coppery iris of the toad in the grass, a heart-shaped pupil absorbs the image of the harbour front. The creature inflates its vocal sac and the vibrations of its larynx emit then a sound, loud croaks that resonate in the tax office like a clock's striking of the hour.

Sometimes I suddenly say the strangest things to my husband, Elisabeth says in accompaniment to the toad.

They just tumble from my mouth. My husband says it is when I am sick. He says that I send him a most diabolical look, that I then have a wide and smiling mouth, and I say— and it is when I am sick that I say this to him . . .

Slowly Elisabeth turns to face the women in the dock. Her red mouth opens like a cherry revealing its sex: How does it happen, little man, that this comes upon me and I become so strange? Perhaps God has permitted that I be held by this peculiar force? Have I forgotten to pray? Now I sense the witches have cast devilry between us, little man. For quite as dear as I formerly held you, quite as horrid you are to me now.

Elisabeth opens wide her eyes; she smiles in surprise at her own mouth, which continues:

When I look upon you, husband, I see the Devil himself. The best for me would be that you walled me up underneath our copper or inside our baking oven.

Slowly she opens her mouth as if in a scream and holds it there a moment, making the croaking of the toad appear to issue from her throat. But she smiles then, and smacks her lips briefly, and, before they curl again in a smile, says:

You may do as you wish with me.

All her teeth are visible.

If you want a wife to disclose to her man everything in sleep, write then the wife's name on a scrap of fresh linen and place this together with the liver of a cockerel underneath her pillow without her knowing, and when asked she will tell you everything she knows.

It is proclaimed that the court will allow to be read out a written testimony given at an earlier time by Apelone Ibsdatter, and a wax child knows what an earlier time means. Someone reads aloud. They say that Apelone admits to having indulged in witchcraft along with Maren Kneppis, Dorte Kjærulf and Christenze Kruckow. That they consulted a black book at night and lit a fire in the rooms and then burned upon it the heart of a bullock. That they stole the good fortunes of others and dealt them out among themselves, and delivered misfortune to several girls in Sæby. And it is read out too that Apelone has confessed that she never encouraged anyone in these nocturnal goings-on, that it was Maren, that it was Christenze and Dorte who were the ringleaders and that she herself merely went along with them out of fear, and that the authorities would do well to punish them that they might then stand cleansed before God when such time comes. Then, Otto asks Apelone if she can confirm what has just been read out as her own testimony. Apelone rises willingly enough, and smiling too, yet words will not come to her. Maren weeps. Christenze is pale. Dorte gnashes her teeth. Otto asks again if Apelone can confirm it.

Confirm what?

That which has just been read.

What about it?

That it is your testimony.

She nods, her mouth still wearing its smile, her broken

front tooth plain to be seen. Apelone, she speaks softly, happily, and says:

I have a secret. There is a herring swimming inside my head. Soon I am going to fly to the sun.

Can you confirm that what you have just heard read is your testimony? Otto says.

Today is a good day for judgement, Apelone says. There are things we know about, all of us. We know a thing or two about the king's lieutenants and prisons and God.

I recognize the talk of a witch when I hear it, says Klyne.

And then I am with Peder Fisker, at his mouth, the darkly stained creases of his fingers, the hand he runs through his hair, his contempt for the clergy, his Klyne-aversion, which sits like cramp about the root of his tongue.

Enough, Klyne, Peder shouts, surprising himself and all around him with the resonance of his voice: Stop this now.

Onlookers press forward, several stumble and fall as they surge in from the doorway, as they jostle to stand before Otto. And there is Peder, and there are Dorte's girls and their husbands, among them Hieronimus the town clerk, they close around Dorte, and then Christenze herself comes forward, and no one stops her, and Apelone's Anders too, he has turned a courtroom before and sees now an opportunity, a trembling moment at which a punishment may be avoided, he steps up in front of the jurors, his trousers too short for the length of his legs.

Can you not see what they have done to my wife? he says. Anyone can tell that she has lost her mind. They have tortured her from her senses and the goodness of her skin.

Peder is warm, he knows what Anders is about, and comes to his aid. I see it happen, it is like a taste to me.

She has been interrogated and painfully tormented, Peder says, I heard the screams myself.

Her confession cannot be valid, Anders says.

And Dorte's girls shove their men forward, they mumble their own protests, and Hieronimus is now standing right before Dorte. Maren's man, Olaf, sits petrified as yet. Karen must tug on his sleeve to waken him from his daze.

Listen now, Manderup ventures, and so speaks for the first time.

Manderup, Otto barks, and no more is required to shut the old man up.

You have gone too far, Peder says.

But the accusation is your own, Otto says, you were the one who first saw them.

I had no idea it would come to this, Peder replies.

Do you renounce the Devil, Peder? Otto asks.

Oh, stop this, says Anders.

And all his works and all the rest of it, says Peder.

Who now remembers Dorte? Who remembers Apelone, Maren and Christenze? The dolls on the row of chairs. The four yellow quinces. Christenze thinks of watercress. Peder speaks as he spoke before when denouncing them, but now in their defence. He is an odd fellow, Christenze thinks, to change his opinion in such a way. Is it really the case that he did not understand how far they would go? All this time, his animosity towards Aalborg's important men has tussled with his fear of witchcraft.

They confessed only when you tortured them, Peder says. Your blood-thirst ran away with you. Do you seriously believe it must end with their burning?

Otto – Manderup again now, his voice a tremble – if we now say the girls have been given their warning, then the matter will be settled and our house will be in order.

Otto leans towards him and speaks to him now in a low voice only I can hear: The king will not accept it. And the old man, eyes wide, nods.

It has already begun. It has already occurred. It may be turned in the hand like a figure, cast or moulded, and considered from wherever one stands.

One day a long time ago, my mistress picked a handful of red clovers where the sheep grazed. She put them in a cup with olive oil and mixed them well, then dabbed my eyes and her own with the mixture as if it was a perfume, and our eyes were made happy by it and danced with joy in our skulls, and we saw clouds hurry by in blues and pinks, and we saw a machine kept moving by a wheel, its rods ensnared and snatched up my mistress, and carried her into the air until she could not escape, while I hung at the fringes like a strange heart sending its seed stems towards her in vain.

Amid this commotion, Klyne observes Dorte as she speaks with her son-in-law. He sees the rope come undone from her hands, and as she lifts her one-eyed face Klyne emits a gasp, for there is recognition in her eye, it sees something no one otherwise sees, something inside him that is not priest, something inside her that is not woman. Her gaze pierces him like a ray of light, light, and she is like a nettle that gently quivers in a breeze. The hairs of his arms stand on end, as if he had burned himself upon her. Her mouth whispers to him, but he cannot hear what she says. Behind him, Manderup and Otto are engaged in argument with the others. Only Klyne sees Hieronimus lead Dorte away through the room, but as she passes him she cannot help herself, but leans in to Klyne and whispers into his ear:

Shall I churn your butter?

Klyne's hand is quicker than his thought – he grips her arm and digs in his nails.

Desist, he bellows, the voice he employs in his sermons, a voice he has refined and which will cause a congregation to cower, and indeed the courtroom falls silent, the tax office is now his church, and the voice says:

These wives are no longer your women, for they have given themselves unto Satan. And Satan laughs at us, can you not hear him? The Devil is about in Aalborg. We stand in the midst of his terrible music, which twists everything from its proper location. Let him enter not.

And then Klyne drags Dorte back through the room to the dock.

Dorte Kjærulf here was about to flee, he says, which in itself is proof of her guilt, he says. Pull yourselves together, men, he says.

Apelone is like a child whose sudden discomposure when encountering a great fright causes her to jump up and down on the spot instead of running away. She shouts:

The church is a strange bride, with the Devil now I shall abide. Maren is the witch!

She laughs a mad and ear-piercing laughter. Screams come together like a fish-shoal of voices beneath the ceiling.

Apelone! Christenze shouts.

There you have it! Klyne shouts.

Order in the court! Manderup shouts, white with fear.

Settle down, Otto commands. Be seated.

And Peder and Anders, Christenze, Dorte's girls, Hieronimus, each and every one acquiesces, while Apelone continues to giggle.

Maren Kneppis Nielsdatter, Otto says, the charges against you have now been laid out and it is time to hear the verdict of the jury.

Like figures carved in wood, the jurors have sat during the entire process with stiff and expressionless faces. Now they turn to each other with a rustle of fabric and their mumbling voices confer. After a short time, the parish priest Gregers Iversen rises. They know him, often he will come to Aalborg to purchase shrimps.

In this case that has been brought against Maren Kneppis, he says, it is the considered opinion of the jury that the accused has failed to repudiate the accusations made against her. For this reason, and in view of much evidence, she should rightly be convicted of witchcraft.

Christenze takes Maren's hand. My mistress tries to think of a new plan, but nothing will hatch, she must start again and again, as if attempting to solve some problem of mathematics from which the crucial information is missing, her thoughts keep getting stuck. Nothing comes to her. For a moment all is still. Then Maren speaks:

I shall go gladly to my death.

Not so fast, Manderup says, the punishment has not yet been handed down.

There is only one punishment for witchcraft, Otto says.

You don't mean that, Manderup says.

I am only following the law, Otto says.

That law is quite new.

A new law is as valid as an old one.

What law? Maren asks.

That all manner of witchcraft shall be punished by burning, Christenze says.

Then the parish priest speaks again:

Since this case is of such serious nature, we shall remind the court that the convicted woman must also have her case tried at the provincial court in Viborg before the matter may be considered concluded.

But what is the sentence? asks Peder, and turns searchingly towards Otto, who stands gazing at the window. Otto is in no hurry. He straightens his shoulders, tilts his head; he takes a deep breath and looks upon the fjord, and then it comes, the moment, it is not a difficult line to cross when you have already ventured this far: he releases fate.

Maren Kneppis Nielsdatter, he says, is hereby sentenced to death by burning.

Shouts go up, the court descends into tumult. It was a peculiar moment for a wax child. There was the knowledge that this was not good for my mistress, but also gladness at the boiling blood that now pervaded the room; that temperatures rose, that every cheek was so vivid and red, that everyone present tasted iron, that the horror had not yet grown cold, that it was thrashing still, that it retained as yet a generative force that could be harnessed and put to use. But this opening is only brief, before the horror becomes a tool in the hands of those who are able to wield it. Hideous Høeg steps forward and grabs hold of Maren. Upon her now are all the widest eyes, in which the sea and the blossoming hawthorn reflect as in a hundred mirrors containing a hundred tiny Maren-shadows. Christenze rises, and Dorte likewise, then Apelone, and Klyne too rises, he almost clambers over the assembled folk in order to get to the women, while Dorte proceeds to loudly pray:

We looked in the east, we looked in the west, we saw

a blood-smeared giant. She bites the neck, she bites the bone, now breaks the stick, now breaks the stone. You take from us our sister.

Klyne strikes Dorte with the flat of his hand. He licks from his palm the spit from her open hag-mouth. It tastes of chicory root and salt and leather.

Shortly afterwards the castle is still. Everyone has gone home. Klyne stands in the corridor, he stands in God's light of early afternoon, and his heart is beating hard. He closes his eyes and raises his arms in the blessing, he does not say a word. There is a whisper as if from angels, a rustling of feathered wings, a single crusty seed in his heart, and he is thirsty, he goes with a determined stride towards the ale-room.

How do I know this? The dead fly in the windowsill told me, the grass-pollen as it puffed into the air told me, a brass candlestick told me, a speck of grit. Everything remembers and speaks to those who will listen.

It starts to hail. It is only a brief shower. The hailstones pummel up a cloud of hawthorn blossom. Afterwards, their ice lies scattered between male-fern and the sun's thin and wavy threads. My mistress has forgotten something on her way back to the cell, it's obvious, it's on the tip of her tongue, but what is it? It has happened already, she is surprised to realize. My mistress once lay down in a tub with many brilliant green shoots of the male-fern, the tips, when they are yet to fully uncurl, but still stand like conches of the undergrowth. What Hideous Høeg tells them on the way back is something she already knows. It is in the depths of her vessels, in that which we call horn and hair. In the smallest sequences it resides there still. I don't need to tell so much, I am merely a reminder, a down that settles upon your brow, and I am with you.

Maren has been afraid a long time now, but as the carriage shakes her like a lentil in a boot, her fear is transformed into indifference, and then peculiar delight. She looks out upon the meadows, the fields, the dew ponds filled with water after the rain. Maren decides she will be a stupid wife. Perhaps she has been one all along. She shrugs off all responsibility. About her brain she wraps a film of lies, so now no one can get to her, and no one can get to Karen or the others. Inside the carriage, the strength of the early summer could almost make her forget where she is being taken. Pigeons coo in the sun. The blackbird is at the peak of its season. There is something intoxicatingly green in the shimmer through which they drive on their way to Viborg; there is beech and ash and oak and apple. Maren says the names to herself of all that she sees outside: nettles, garlic mustard, cranesbills, spurge, and the cuckoo calls, and then suddenly there are linden trees before her, whose midsummer scent she will not smell again.

Someone said: Are we really in the Devil's golden age as they say we are? What do they say? What did he say? He said that a witch is the Devil's milk-maid, and she milks him and he milks her, and they milk each other all the way to the pit of Hell. And they said, what did they say? Some said that the Devil's sacraments show themselves as symbols and figures, images, and in the misuse of all manner of things – as salt, soil, ribbon, paper, wax, thread, scissors, coin, nails, hair, the foreheads of the dead, teeth and bones, altar wine, baptismal water and the wax of church candles. Someone said: Even the king drinks strong ale. I saw they had marzipan pears on the market square; no, I heard they had bitter oranges after dinner at the mayor's house. Don't be stupid, someone said, the law is meant to be the same for everyone, the same law to apply overall. Clever folk follow the law, employ the law to resolve their disputes, someone said, and someone said: Will the king come to Aalborg? No, I think not. He is to attend the celebratory service in Sealand. He is to celebrate the Lutheran jubilee. That is what he will do. But it is a long time ago now. He exhibits his dry blood, and then the blood is brown.

It is almost June and outside their cell they can hear jeering and the chopping of an axe. It is the carpenter, who is making the ladder for Maren. They have not seen her in two weeks now. Then they smell the smoke, and then Otto Skeel is reading aloud Maren's confession. Then the screams. No. I will not hear it. There is a smell of human flesh. In front of the bonfire, Karen stands with me upon her arm. Maren is tied to the ladder, and the ladder pushed into the bonfire. As it falls, the ladder turns and Maren falls backwards into the flames. Karen stands with her father's hand upon her shoulder. She will be ten years old this summer. Her mother coughs. Then Maren's body becomes limp, though her eyes are open. Karen sees her mother's eye become so strangely orange from within. And then in the heat it explodes. Her father gasps. Karen clutches me to her breast as she watches the bonfire. She says: Fuck shit piss the Devil's piss shit fuck piss shit the Devil's fucking hell hell hell.

If you want to quell a fire, you must speak to it and say, *Be still in your breath, as Jesus stilled into death. By his five wonders red, be still upon your bed. By the Virgin's cheeks, ruddy and round, with Sulfanus be bound. Your red wings subdue. I bid you fire, which burns here, be snuffed.*

Come here, my girl.

It is Apelone who calls. Karen has come to the casemates with her wax child, in the forenoon. Months have passed since the morning of their arrest. Soon it will be midsummer. There is warmth now at the pit of twelve o'clock, a pear of light and syrup, which Karen normally will greedily ingest, but since that day she has not been hungry and has been dry in her eyes, as if she was a creature that has ceased to sleep. In the crack between wall and door Karen sees a pale mouth shape the words:

Come here, my girl.

They say Apelone has gone mad. That you can hear her scream and laugh at night, if you walk along Slotsgade.

Come here, my girl, I have something to tell you, she says. Closer now, that's right. I have a message to you from your mother. Come, put your ear to the crack so that you can hear me better, and let me tell you what your mother told me: There is said to be a stone in the right hind leg of a hedgehog, the size of a barley grain, and the stone shall be taken in the name of Figirum, Figulatum and Belsebub; when you have it taken you shall be hardened so that neither sword nor dagger can pierce you. The young of the raven are known to be white when hatched from the egg, and the nest is filled with carrion and becomes infested with maggots on which the young will feed for a month. In that time the raven flies from its young and will not care to look at them for as long as they are white. A black dog came to me, such a lively fellow, with a red cape of velvet and a grand moustache, and he said he could teach me to churn butter so there would always be more in the churn, and he said he could make himself invisible, which I then wished to learn also, and so he said to me, You are to go to the swallow's nest in the barn on a Thursday and have with you an awl, and you are to pierce the head of each of the young from one eye to the other. On the following Thursday go there again and look and you will find a stone beside each of the young when you shake their wings, for the stones are concealed beneath them. And he made me do it, Karen, I was no more than sixteen years old, a long time ago now. I went with the awl in my hand to a nest of young and put out their eyes. The following Thursday I went there again and looked into the nest. But there were the young with eyes as good and clear as before and could see with them. I knew though that I had put them out with the awl. And then about my head, suddenly, something like a cobweb was spun and a mist clouded my eyes, causing me almost to fall from the ladder. So then it was begun, I can tell you. I have often thought of how great a sin that fellow made me commit. I would sit and read in his book, which he had lent to me, whenever I had a moment, but Anders noticed this and raised his stick and threatened me, saying that if truth did not come from my lips, I would be beaten. But then I told him that I could churn butter and that I could give to him, little by little, good fortune and gold, these things would come to him soon. Have you spoken to Anders? How is he? Why does he not visit us? Come closer, Karen, do not run, my little swallow, dear little rat-pup, come here and let me kiss you. Would you like to learn how to churn butter so that the churn will always provide? Do you wish to see the wide world? Shall I teach you to fly?

I am a root, the moon, the stupid thing in your hand when you barter, money in coin, me. No one wants to eat me, but I am here for consuming. I was made a delicacy of shadows. Give to me not what you give me: eyes, attention, thoughts. I will have meat, human blood, a field of skin. The warmth that belongs to the first-born under the willing arm, insufferable softness. Go to my lying-place, I am awake. I begin to believe I need a mistress in order to prosper. Whoever reads this, said inside their skull by a voice that sounds like mine, shall be my mistress, my needle. I, a part of the Earth's crust, broken away and now in your hand, while in your mind you hold me, as though newborn.

Whenever Karen visited the casemates to whisper with Dorte and the others, she would lay me down on the ground at the foot of the door; there, the earth would scuff me, mud would mottle me, an insect might briefly settle, a worm wriggle at my side, and as the weather grew warmer, fluff and seed would cling to my wax, and then perhaps again be taken by a wind, and spores danced in the air. But the best to talk to was a chaffinch that had made its nest in a tall tree in the castle yard, and though earth and spores had much to tell, it was the chaffinch that knew best what had happened to my mistress and her companions, and vividly, with great narrative skill, the bird passed on to me the following: It was some few days after Maren's demise, one forenoon, I think, damp and foggy, and a man came to the entrance of the casemates to ask for admittance. They heard Hideous Høeg turn the keys in the locks, and my friend the chaffinch saw that those imprisoned knew that the visitor was Klyne. All the birds of Aalborg knew Klyne. Even many animals of the town were acquainted with his rage. Now Klyne's face had put on a gentle air and he brought with him sweetbreads and wine. A chair was carried in, and a table at which he could sit. The three women were seated on the earthen floor, leaning back against a wall. Klyne poured wine into a slender glass. His thumbnail squeaked to me later that Klyne found the women to resemble three rag dolls sat in a row, their legs splayed out in front of them, their arms hung limply at their sides, three slack mouths breathing in a thick and foul-smelling air.

I have been asked by the mayors and council to visit you in the capacity of my office, he said, to comfort you and to urge you to tell the truth in confession.

No one spoke. They stared at the bread. He broke pieces from the loaf and approached them. Here, the chaffinch commented that this in particular made an impression on her, since the three inmates appeared thereby to occupy a role familiar to birds, waiting for a human to scatter crumbs. Klyne smoothed his hand over Apelone's cheek; like a weary child she accepted his caress.

How are you? he asked.

Not very well, Apelone said.

Come with me, he said, and helped Apelone to her feet and sat her on his chair.

How is your wife? Dorte asked from her place on the ground.

I really am sorry, Apelone said to Klyne.

What do you mean? he asked.

She became so . . . we were mean to her.

We were not, Dorte said.

She has suffered a great deal, Klyne said.

Now it comes over Apelone again, and she shakes herself like a cat, as if something had at that moment scurried up and down inside her, underneath her skin. Like when someone has worms, as my chaffinch described it. And from Apelone there comes a shrill and rasping voice that does not resemble her own:

My little servant boy told me. His name is Raggi. Christenze too has a little boy.

What boys are you talking about? Klyne asked.

Our little help-mates from Hell, our helping devils. Christenze's is called Jeronymus. Dorte's is Plugie. Christenze and Dorte were in your church at night to cast a spell upon Elisabeth. It was their idea, not mine at all. The pissing and shitting outside the mayor's house was all Christenze's doing. She is indeed busy with such things, also that which I know nothing about, or cannot quite remember.

Dear God, Klyne said. Go on.

But Christenze has always resented many men of the town, she is unfamiliar with men-folk. I asked her why we had to shit at the mayor's door and she said that since we had pissed there the previous night, we should then shit there too, and then she laughed it off and said it really was no concern of mine. They were the ones who wanted it done. I was a part of it, but it was not my idea.

Let me bless you, my child, Klyne said, visibly shaken, and took from his pocket a Bible. He licked his fingers to turn the flimsy pages.

You have learned their story well, Dorte said to Apelone.

Christenze rose and stepped over to the table, she bent down and whispered in Apelone's ear, though loud enough for Klyne to hear:

Take no heed of what he says. I shall look after you and help you out of here.

And Apelone on the chair turned to face her and

threw her arms around her waist, and buried her face in her skirts to weep. Klyne considered them.

If this is where it is leading, then I have nothing to do here, he said. But I have need of the table and chair when I leave.

He knocked on the door to signal to Hideous Høeg that he should come and let him out.

On your feet, he said to Apelone, who as yet clutched Christenze who was standing before her. Klyne sought to pull Apelone away, she hissed and scratched his arm, he struck her in the face, Christenze shoved him, which caused him to fall and put his hand in human excrement. Appalled, he scrambled to his feet and approached Christenze, Hideous Høeg rattled at the door, and the pastor Klyne head-butted Christenze, who dropped to the floor. Blood ran from her hairline, she was unconscious. Now Dorte came from behind and jumped upon Klyne and dug her fingers into his eyes, he screamed, and Hideous Høeg pulled her from him. Apelone was still sitting on the chair, sobbing. Hideous Høeg held Dorte in his grasp and his hand groped about her.

What is this? he said, and reached inside her dress to retrieve something from Dorte's armpit.

It was a small packet, made from a sheet of paper folded into a small triangle. A strange calm descended upon everyone in the cell, as if they stood upon a ship sailing either into or out of the night, as if together they had stepped through a crevice into a warm and sun-drenched glen where no person before them had ever been. Light spilled in through the open door, spilled upon Apelone, who narrowed her eyes. Hideous Høeg tossed the packet on to the table, Klyne opened it carefully. The paper contained a blue headscarf.

It is Elisabeth's, Klyne said, meticulously unfolding the scarf. Apelone rose and went towards the light. She paused, put her hand against the doorframe, and realized then that no one had seen her. She stepped out into the deserted yard, turning her face to the sky.

Inside the scarf was another small packet, containing hair. Klyne teased the hair apart to find yet another, even smaller paper packet, and this likewise he removed and unfolded.

In the middle of the yard was a tree, that of the chaffinch. Apelone placed a hand against it and curled around the trunk.

What does it say? said Hideous Høeg.

Klyne read out loud:

This scarf was given to me by Elisabeth on the Sunday after the Saturday when she and many others spoke falsely about me at Aalborghus Castle. Yet with God's help nothing of what was said will hurt me, and they will reap only as they have sown.

Hideous Høeg and Klyne looked at Dorte.

Did you write this? Klyne asked.

Are you stupid? Dorte hissed. Do you not think I know a little witchcraft?

Klyne dropped the amulet as if it was burning hot and darted at once from the cell.

Apelone, Hideous Høeg shouted out, come back in here so I can lock up.

He took away the table and chair, the bread and the wine, with a lightness about him. Apelone trudged back inside and smiled at him before he locked the door. As he turned to leave, he heard her voice say: Thanks for your time today.

I saw him build the first workhouse, the first reformatory, and establish a new city quarter. I saw him erect the Round Tower, the new houses of Nyboder, Frederiksborg Castle, and what is called Oslo. I saw him organize into a single fortress the countries over which he ruled. I saw him ride, conduct war, and preen himself. I saw him proclaim Copenhagen as the country's first capital, and lay down the borders of Denmark and Norway. I saw him in crimson, I saw him in gold. I saw his Colour Chamber, his Treasury, his secret toilet. I saw his myth as it grew, his moustache waxed with lard. I saw the king's stomach bulge behind the gleaming buttons of his coat. I saw him send his ships to Tranquebar and Finnmark and establish a trading monopoly in Iceland. I saw him lay claim to new territories, to Arctic waters. I saw him legislate against witchcraft and promiscuity, against costly weddings, against drunkenness, opulent dressing, and inns. I saw him issue warrants to commandeer adolescent boys who had not yet learned a trade from their parents. I see him impose taxes, and introduce agrarian reforms and trade legislation. I see him have his slippers embroidered. I see him demonstrate his kingship, I see a benign cyst upon his liver. I see a vessel brimming with blood. I see the first prison. I see him receive the information that Galileo has observed the moons of Jupiter. I see his horoscope be cast. I see him observe the face of Las Thomsen as the light in Galten falls upon him and Las is sentenced to pay a fine of fifty rigsdaler for the rape of Maren Nielsdatter, I see in his nose the smell of

Las's stained coat, the image of a cellar, of bare feet and stagnant water. I see him collapse into a chair when a war is over. I see his crest partly covered with snow on the west coast of Greenland. I see him drink from the tooth of a whale. In a fleeting moment one morning in May the world is changed. Gulls screech and soar above the city. It is trial-time, axe-time. A time for fire and fury. Time turns sleepily with corpses in its coat. You make money. Children come out of other children. Violet-blue waters lap against warm sandbanks. You are not, and should not, be appeased. You do not know yourselves. I see him build the Collegium Regium, the Stock Market, Rosenborg Castle. I see the big dye-houses produce uniforms for the Navy, I see the beginnings of a silk industry, I see the beginnings of an African company. I see him set up the postal service.

I was the wax child. The thorn-apple resembles me. Needle-filled and with possibilities as yet unexpressed. As the thorn-apple opens its mouth, like the chestnut at first a pair of lips of whitish flesh, the teeth then appear in the aperture, densely and disorderly set, like grains of yellow rice, lentils bared and growling. I wonder what a cross-section of me would reveal? Certain seeds and blades of straw; perhaps, as often in amber, insects; teeth and hair, fingernails, spikes; this unuttered excess in her thoughtless presence.

Anne Christensdatter visited, on the Saturday afternoon before Christmas, Anders Guldsmed's shop. There stood Jens, and it is he who now tells it to Otto, for the king has issued an open letter to the citizens of Aalborg, urging them to disclose whatever they may have heard or seen in the matter of the scourge that blights North Jutland, anything that concerns the society of witches that has been centered around Jomfru Christenze Axelsdatter Kruckow, and stating that they ought now to step forward, if they are good men and citizens, and say what they know, and Jens Pedersen is young, around twenty years of age, though his hair is already receding on his glistening forehead, and he is soon to be married, this he has learned in the cellar, for they went down into it one at a time in the days of Christmas and there had been put a table by the young lads and girls of the quarter, and on the table were three cups, one containing water, one containing ordinary ale, and one of strong ale. With eyes closed, each entered the cellar room alone, and stepped to the table and chose without seeing a cup from which to drink, and Jens tasted the good and mild ale and opened then his eyes at once, and the entire damp-smelling room glowed with a golden light as if a thousand candles had been lit, and a beautiful young woman moved towards him and he knew then that in the coming year he would be wed. And now he sits on a chair before Otto Skeel and tells him about Anne, who is a servant girl in the house of Anders and Apelone, the same house in which he serves, and how this Anne Christensdatter one Saturday evening before Christmas asked him to go up with her to Anders's chamber and asked if he wanted to see something on the condition he could keep quiet about it, and when he promised this, she took out Anders's uniform and showed him that there hung a small white pouch inside the right arm, at the armpit, and she shook the pouch and asked Jens, What sort of pepper pouch do you think this is? And Jens had no idea and could not explain why Anders would have it about his person, but then he squeezed it and felt that it was filled with paper, so Anne Christensdatter and Jens, that Saturday before Christmas, took the uniform into the scullery, where they picked open the pouch, and all this is what Jens tells to Otto, who maintains the proper and interested expression, and all this travelled through the town along my channels, was brought to me by my messengers, I who used my spine by which to listen, and inside the pouch, this Saturday evening before Christmas, in the dim light shortly after the winter solstice, midwinter, and in the golden shimmer of living, tamed fire, and the warm snorting of living livestock, and the wind skimming over the fjord, blustering, as cattle running, in the pouch they found a letter, a note folded about another note, which formed a triangle and bore the written names of folk they knew and knew that Anders knew, and the names were written crosswise and back to front, and on the paper were drawn nine crosses, one in each corner, on each side and in the middle. Underneath the names it was written that these persons shall deal kindly with me, Anders Guldsmed, that they shall not in any way harm my property or money, my honour or reputation, but be so well disposed towards me as the Virgin Mary to her own infant, this is what was written, what they read, what he says, what I am saying now, what is written here, the very words.

One of these lonely teeth, a cheek-tooth extracted, which over time had travelled through my wax, along the length of my thigh, we shared in not having proper mouths, but despite this deficiency the tooth would often sing the same song from its place in my thigh: I have no power. I have no courage. I saw the lark descend. I will love in vain for ever. Hidden in me are her calcium and old blood vessels and nerves. If I could eat a cake made in the shape of her left breast, I would do it. I would lick her from head to toe. If I had a human tongue, I would do it. But I am worth nothing to her. I would do anything to soften her, seduce her and allow her most secret of sighs to escape in my presence. But it will never happen, and it does not hurt. I am a tooth. My craving is my fuel, a journey in another life. My love is not made for happiness, but for longing. I am worth nothing to her.

Do you believe a sick person can be healed by crawling through the roots of a full-grown willow?

I don't know.

Do you believe a bottle of wine that has been buried in the ground to be a more effective medicine than other wine?

I really could not say.

Do you believe a person may be cured of a sickness by eating paper cuttings on a slice of bread?

I have no idea.

Was the Devil, when you lay with him, warm or cold?

Neither.

What are you doing?

I would like to return to the cell.

Where are the others? My mistress asks, for she sees now that she is alone in the cell. Hideous Høeg, who brings her food and water, says:

They are on their way to Viborg.

What for?

To be tried for witchcraft at the provincial court after they were found guilty here.

They have been found guilty? When?

Do you not remember?

I am still waiting for you to understand that you have made a mistake.

A person could almost feel sorry for you, he mutters.

What day is it? she asks.

Monday.

Already?

Yes.

Do you know why I have these wounds on my wrists and here too on my ankles?

Don't work your witchcraft on me. You know perfectly well what has gone on.

No, I don't. Tell me, please. Where are the others?

Gone to court, I already said.

Of course, yes. Do you think they will be acquitted?

Her face is open like he has never seen it before, an openness they have sought for so long in their examinations of her, but she is always so spiteful then. Now she is like the violet. Straight as a child and close to the ground. How do I know this? It is like a gash in me to know it. He holds water to her mouth, and she drinks gratefully.

Things will get better soon, will they not? she asks. Can you not ask them to release me?

But, he asks, have you not committed acts of witchcraft as they say?

Is that what they say?

Yes.

What is it they say? she asks.

Well, all manner of things. That you have lain with the Devil and bewitched Klyne's wife.

Elisabeth?

Yes, her.

You know that I am noble?

Yes.

Then you must understand that you have made a mistake. I must be released. Where is Anders? Where is Peder? Have they not come? Where is Maren?

Enough. He gets to his feet. She closes her eyes.

Ah, yes, that's right, she says, cross-legged in the dust, now I remember. It was Lucia night. I remember now. One must fill a shoe with wine or ale and walk very quickly, without the feet beginning to sweat.

She opens her eyes and he sees that she is returned.

Don't do anything stupid while you are on your own, he says.

I love life, she says, it belongs to me.

A person, levitating, lifting their arms, mouth widened in fright, though no scream is forthcoming, the bonfire that burns him is made of stalks and butterwort, of common bladderwort and slender, glistening leaves like the eyes of a reptile, of glands and fly-traps, such an image, from hillside and mountainside, red ochre blended into skimmed milk, the near-erotic paintbrush that is taken from the bucket's tawny mixture, the opaque water running from the bristles of the brush back into the bucket, like Samson prising open the jaws of the lion, or an angel, haloed, wrapping its arms around the lion's neck, pouring water from a beaker into a spring, the spring pouring it back into the beaker, an infinite letter.

The swallow keeps in its stomach a stone, a gastrolite is what it is, and yet at the same time an amulet, storied like wax children. The stone, the size of a lentil, may be placed in the corner of the eye of a person whose eye is sick, and the stone will stick to the orb and then travel under the lid and bring immediate relief; tears will lubricate its path over the mucous membrane, there is no discomfort, and the swallow-stone may later be removed and used again on others.

The swallow-stone is concave and therefore extremely delicate, its edges are pale grey in colour, whereas its hollow is dark purple and speckled.

What did it have to tell me?

A dark chamber beneath the ground.

That was all it said.

It was neither good nor bad, but quite beyond the

principles of morality. It was as if this lightless chamber vibrated. And I knew not whether it was something that already existed, had been lost, or was to come. There was no more to be said about it than that. It was the language and utterance of the swallow-stone: *A dark, vibrating, underground chamber.*

Help me, my mistress slurred, the king is coming. I am at the outskirts of the shoal.

She was dreaming, and I, who often dreamt, though never slept, heard her from my place in Karen's chamber. Her smell rose and travelled far from her cell, and filled the room. It was a rank smell of fear and sweat, of shame and repentance, the sweet smell of internal blood. The smell of open, unwashed genitals.

We are swimming upwards to the sun, she said in her sleep, the sun is a god beneath the sea too.

They burned Apelone on the second of June, on the wooded hill in the city. A light rain fell. When it cleared, the birds sang; the fire caught well, and burned quickly. Bound to her ladder, she laughed and said, Paradise, here I come.

Her lavender-grey skirt, shiny from wear, flamed into a blazing ball.

Dorte was burned two days later, the fourth of June, at the same place. On this occasion, the flames refused to catch at first and the fire went out. The night-man went again to light it. Dorte looked down on him from her ladder. Then the fire took hold. It was clear to everyone that the moment had come and that Dorte would get to speak her final words. The bonfire flared into a blaze and grew so hot one had to step back. The two men holding Dorte's ladder (coffin, I nearly said) narrowed their eyes as the heat stung their faces. Dorte looked around at those who were gathered and saw that they were as if paralysed by it. In her cell, Christenze heard Dorte shout, and she cried for the first time. It was early in my dream, I was but a child, I was new to the world, freshly broken from the whole to be a single part. Now I am new no more, I am decidedly worn out. I know of one like me, older and not of wax, but pouched in form and made of leather, who inside them carries the talon of a goshawk, the tip of a grass snake's tail, a whole shell of the whelk and a sliver of broken mussel-shell, specks of grit in a pigeon's gut, and the lower jawbone of a squirrel. Some things can withstand fire. Iron, certain precious stones, and gold, so in the embers of a bonfire on which a person has been burned, these things will remain. A thing of wax would melt immediately. A sweet odour, if you melt me down, of honey, clay-soil, a feeling somewhere between lupins and butter. Unhurried, the wax seeped from the scales of the bee; the insect settled among the rosemary and found its balance, before parts of me detached from its abdomen. A thing of wax, brought into the world at first by bees, then by the beekeeper, then by my mistress, in the kitchen that time, when she was like night-water of which to drink, a glittering pool.

Now my mouth opens, and the fingernails then speak, the hair speaks, the horn speaks, and the teeth, the visible part of the skeleton, the bony elements: They said of us that the Devil had come to us in the shape of a large and headless man. They said that he asked us if we were sleeping, and we answered, We are neither sleeping nor awake. They said that he promised us good fortune in all our endeavours, if only we would accept from him a bunch of keys. And they said of us that ever since then the Devil tormented us if we would not perform his evil. That he stretched our limbs until blood ran from our noses and mouths. And it was one of us, Maren Kneppis. Accused of having cast witchcraft upon several persons, thereby causing them sickness and death. Found guilty of witchcraft by the provincial court in 1621 and sentenced to death by burning.

And they said of us that Satan came to us in the peat field and told us that we were to go with him. That he came to us on Christmas night and was horned and shaggy in his appearance, and that he went with us for half a day, whereafter we became exceedingly heavy. That we followed him and forty other witches to Rold Forest, and drank and sang in the hilly moorland known as Rebild Bakker. That we took salt with us into the church on a Sunday and with it did cure a sick person. And they said of us that we could not cry. That this was because the Evil One had bound our tears. And it was one of us, Apelone Ibsdatter. Accused of having cast witchcraft upon several persons, thereby causing them sickness and death. Found guilty of witchcraft by the provincial court in 1621 and sentenced to death by burning.

And they asked us if we had learned sorcery from Christenze Kruckow. Yes! we said. Yes! Get that screw away, remove it. And Maren was already dead. And they asked us if that sorcery was imparted to us in a porridge, during the period of lying-in. And they asked if it was a very thin and mealy porridge in which we found something black which was the size of a barley corn. And if we began to feel pain for some fortnight or more after we had eaten the porridge. Yes! we replied. Yes! After eating the porridge. And they asked us if Satan had come to us in the shape of a cat three weeks after our lying-in. And if he darted up and down the length of our body from feet to mouth, where he counted the teeth. Yes! we replied. He counted the teeth. And they asked us if he came in the shape of a bud that grew upon a twig. And if we gave him one of our fingers in assurance. And if he commanded us to milk the cattle, which belonged to others, and to steal from others their good fortune. Yes! we replied, yes! He was in the shape of a bud which steals the good fortune of others. And it was one of us, Dorte Kjærulf. Accused of having cast witchcraft upon several persons, thereby causing them sickness and death. Found guilty of witchcraft by the provincial court in 1621 and sentenced to death by burning.

One to be hanged drowns not.

One to conjure must stand with the right shoulder open.

It's no art to call upon the bastard, but it's an art to make him leave.

Expect the help from a gruff, a foul-mouthed, a screaming hag.

Silence, as she alters you.

Soil from a grave in a rag on the chest. Burial of the linen of the sick in a place where the sun never comes.

Bloody milk of the sick cow upon the ant-hill. Oil in water, fox-teeth by the mouth of the child, flesh and blood of Christ in the fist, under the palate, a yearning, a whole never made light, a fray-boggard, the rosemary bush – dust-covered, kingly in its anticipation, every smallest lance-shaped leaf.

Today, which is the fearful Friday, I pronounce woe and damnation upon you all and upon the town of Aalborg. You, who have taken away the lives of good women who have never shown you anything but solicitude. All your ways and deeds shall be accursed. You shall be afraid and downcast and never find rest in this world until you repent that which you now bring about. The Lord shall punish you with madness, syphilis, leprosy and jaundice. When you seek counsel and comfort, you shall never find it. The wrath of the Lord shall consume you like devouring fire, and all God's curses and suffering shall come upon you. And all that you hold in your hands shall be accursed. You shall wake up anxious and afraid, and sleep with unhappiness and sorrow. Heaven and Earth shall bedamn you, until you confess what you have done here. The fish in the sea and the animals that crawl upon the field shall call upon you burden and calamity. Leaf and grass and all that the soil does bear shall condemn you, and your gladness shall be turned into grief and tears. You shall plough and sow, but worms and grasshoppers shall reap your crops. You shall be drained of all moisture, and wither then like trees, and wizen like grass, and no one shall find way to your abode. You shall build and plant, yet the fire and fury of the Lord shall disrupt you. You shall live and be afraid, and no one shall comfort you. The torments of Hell and eternal damnation shall be your wage. Your town shall be damned, and your farms and properties, your fields and meadows. Damned shall be your tongues, damned shall be your hands and feet, damned shall be your bodies and souls, until you are able to comprehend what by these deeds you have done unto your poor neighbours.

It would have been easier to think that she had been dead for some time than to remember nothing, even though she has been alive the whole time. It was hard to grasp where the others were. A flea sprang upon a hand that rested in her lap, in order to drink. It was night, but it was early summer, but it was still December in the cell, as if time had never passed. What was the time even when they took her? When they came for her, and the screws, the marks they left, the openings into which the fleas would bury. Four lives in a flea, pardoned, held. A living temple upon a floor of stamped earth, the ground, these walls, this stone structure inside an earthen mound, where swallows build their nests, hatch their young. She squeezed the flea between two fingers and her fingernail was squirted purple by the blood of those most dear. Girlfriends. The taste of crocus – iron – sparkles of stars – there is something out there whose eye is upon her, she who is to be rigorously examined. Make a child of wax, by the mandrake's root. Back when the day was a happy day; these rags of time, and in them the sun's twin resides, a pear's light-drenched flesh; to go further, backwards into the white summer's night, to a crossroads, to heathen ground, lilac-coloured. A person falls like a drop of oil in a room, is thrown into a tub of water. Those who knew what happened were obliged to make way for those who know so little. And less than little. And eventually as little as nothing. When was I happy? When I was with her. When I resonated with her tone. When she looked at me with love; when I obtained her secrets, soft and slippery. Wild flowers have spread upon the mound in the woods, later they are mown and give way to grass. Someone must be stretched, like skin upon the wheel. Someone must take the punishment, when punishment is handed down. Cow parsley, yarrow, comfrey in the mouth, and the mouth peers up at the stars. Eyes listen. The nose, our king, tastes everything.

And I was in the king's ear, and I was in the king's mouth, he would go on to live for many more years, and try out many eiderdowns, and he wrote: With regard to the society of witches in North Jutland, it is our will that Christenze Kruckow be rigorously examined and that you not hasten in her execution, that more may be learned about her exploits. Moreover, it has come to our attention that a number of citizens of our borough of Aalborg have endeavoured to prevent the trial of said witches from proceeding, and we instruct you therefore according to our will, that you bring charges against and punish those responsible for said interruption, that the inviolable authority of the court thereby may be protected. Finally, we attach for you, Otto Skeel, a summons and wish that you read it aloud to Jomfru Christenze Axelsdatter Kruckow, whom in accordance with our instruction you have arrested and imprisoned. Announce this to her and come then to the Herredagen assembly here in Copenhagen with her and the documents pertaining to her case, and bring also the priest who has put forward the charges, that we may put this noblewoman before the court.

Karen snatched me up in Aalborg, she brushed the straw from my face, for I had lain in her bed a long time. She ran through town, her child-heart raced, I drank its warm pulse, she caught up to a carriage and handed me in through its window. There sat Otto and Klyne and Elisabeth, but also my mistress, Christenze, and Karen cried out as we set off towards Copenhagen: We'll see each other in Paradise!

Perhaps still one of the happiest moments was when I lay inside a room of Maren's house and could hear my mistress and her coven practising a song in the kitchen below, their voices a babble of good-humoured gossip and chat, at intervals coming together as one, a single voice in song, and there I lay, enraptured, in sunlight, listening to their voices ebbing and flowing, over and over, until I heard a step upon the stair and Christenze came in, beaming, elated, flushed and at her loveliest, and put her hands on my cheeks, this way, like this, and looked at me warmly, hugged me and spoke to me with sweet words she knew would delight me. There, in the safety of that room, with the reassuring sounds of the women downstairs, everything was good, and I have since listened intently, searched with the ear, for something similar, but I've never found it, perhaps because of my own shortcomings, my own absent inner ear, my lack of marrow.

It was early in my dream. I was the wax child. Forgiveness did not interest me. Cooperation did not interest me. Water would flow as blood in the moat, in the castle lake, and it is Frederiksborg Castle in Copenhagen of which I speak. It is a matter of a simple reversal. One reaches a point of possibility where everything may be integrated into the voice. Certain wishes, certain whims, certain mediocre ideas were pressed into me with pins, and I . . . I had to . . . I had no choice, I could only oblige. And from this enforced and unavoidable obedience sprang my contempt for and love of human beings. One ought to ask the oracle a question inviting a lengthy reply. One ought to ask me questions designed to enlarge me. Visitors to the castle could not resist carving their initials and the year in the chapel's left balustrade, in the soft stone furthest from the altar, and, with diamond rings, in the window glass, and on the leaded panes it still reads:

Hilda 1864
Christina Wald 1663
Mette 2 years

These names, throughout the castle, an urge of the common people to leave a mark upon the house of power, to write, carve one's name in stone or glass, the castle overwritten with words, to say: I was here among the golden orbs and crimson robes of the king; do not believe I did not see the world, do not believe I was of less importance than him, whose self-congratulation did tower above the city, my small name, my trembling signature, glows like a flame in his shadow.

When the carriage arrives in Copenhagen on the fourteenth of June 1621, we make directly for the prison of Copenhagen Castle. It's hot, and we turn down Vimmelskaftet, continue towards the square that is Amagertorv, and swing then in the direction of Slotsholmen. No one speaks. There is an endless sun. Inside the carriage, the dust of Aalborg's summer lingers still, but now the sounds of Copenhagen reach us, drunken cries, the swish of velvet robes, nasal sneezes snorting into a moustache, the cling-clang of naval weapons. At the castle, the master of the tower stands ready to receive Christenze and me. His name is Niels. He speaks briefly with Otto, who then climbs back into the carriage and drives away. Christenze follows Niels. I sit snugly in her pocket. She feels her way with her face, it seems, as if the air was a tangible material, a kind of jelly, or water through which she walks. Niels lowers her down into the Blue Tower by means of a slender rope. Down there is a platform constructed from planks, somewhat in the manner of a raft. Surrounding it is a deep drainage channel whose dark water runs away into the moat. It is not possible to scale the walls, the Blue Tower is as slippery as the inside of an egg. Rats swim about; their teeth click together. Light from the opening above drops through the shaft and settles upon her, until the lid is shifted into place. Then it is dark.

She is unsure, but I know that we sat there for three days and nights, and I sensed that during that time she was in good spirit.

The first night, she dreams that an angel with rat's teeth and a rat's mouth comes to her in the hole. In one hand the angel holds a flaming sword, the other smooths Christenze's hair, and then the angel opens its rat's mouth and out falls a human heart, but it is roasted, and Christenze eats it and is filled by a blessed peace, as if something lovely had been there. She wakes when a spider crawls at the corner of her mouth. She allows it to crawl inside then bites down, a small amount of fluid comes out; she is hungry.

The next night, the rat-angel comes to her again, and she sees how the king himself is about to raise a sword above her head, but the rat-angel's flaming sword is the quicker and chops off the king's head, and the head rolls into her lap and cries up at her like a hungry infant.

The third night, no angel comes. She is cold and trembles with fever. Anne Bille steps from the darkness and kneels before her, she lifts Christenze's skirts and kisses her between her legs, then begins to eat her. And Anne Bille's eyes are two dried yellow flower heads that keep falling out to be replaced by new ones, and the rats decorate themselves with the dried flowers, and Christenze is their queen, she exists to be eaten, she is one with the Blue Tower, and her blood veins unfold, tentacle-like, towards the drainage channel that surrounds her, and continue out into the city's canal system, in its gutters and waste pits she senses the city's breathing, and the smells are of sulphur and lavender and excrement, Copenhagen is cabbage-like, a cabbage plant, its large and curly leaves strive playfully towards the clouds, screeching swallows swarm, blue water above them.

Then it starts to come out of her: I want to speak to the king! I demand to speak to the king. My noble blood commands it!

The lid is lifted away with a grating noise and the shaft of light falls upon her, the rope is thrown down, and she clings to it as they hoist her up. The tower-master, in the company of a heavily pregnant woman wearing fine clothes, receives her.

Curtsy before your mistress, the woman says, and Christenze curtsies. I am the king's wife, my name is Kirsten. I am about to leave for Hillerød to give birth there soon, and they say you know a thing or two. Have you any advice for heartburn?

You should take a communion wafer to eat while sitting up in bed before going to sleep, and then swallow a spoonful of sheep's milk, Christenze says, rubbing her cheek, for it seems to her as if her time inside the dungeon is concentrated there.

And if I want the child to come soon? Kirsten asks.

Take a bath in warm water in which lad's love leaves have been steeped for some time. And then masturbate in the bath.

Niels, Master of the Tower, does not say a word.

That is no more than any other wife in the city could have told me. I thought you were a witch?

Christenze shrugs:

Yes, that is what they tell me.

Come, I will take you to him. With difficulty, the pregnant noblewoman goes through the castle and Christenze follows. Kirsten halts at a closed door.

Christenze senses herself that she has a wild look in her eyes.

What should I say to him?

Allow him to see your noble grace, then perhaps you will have a chance, Kirsten replies, and leaves her.

Christenze regards herself in a large mirror, a shabby dress with a person inside, and the face is too small for the head. She straightens her shoulders, smooths her hair, puts her hand on the cold door knob, and steps inside.

An empty hall. At first, she does not think anyone is there. Then she sees three figures seated on a bench against the wall, waiting. It is Otto, Elisabeth and Klyne.

Is it you? Elisabeth says.

Who else? Christenze replies. Is he here?

Not yet, Otto says.

Why are you all here?

We are to be here until punishment has been served, Klyne says while looking through the window. He wrings his hands.

What do you mean, until punishment has been served?

The Mistress has been sentenced while in the hole, Elisabeth says.

Is that allowed? Christenze asks falteringly, and sits down beside Elisabeth. What is my punishment?

Perhaps it is not for me to . . .

Tell me.

Elisabeth can barely pronounce the words:

The Mistress is to be beheaded on the twenty-sixth of June.

Christenze's mouth is shaped as if she has just tasted a fine spoonful of honey.

The twenty-sixth?

When is he coming? Klyne asks, still wringing his hands.

Patience, my good Klyne, Otto says.

A woman will watch over you until . . . Elisabeth says, her voice trailing off.

What is there to watch for? Klyne asks.

She will see that you do not end your days before time, Elisabeth says.

Calm now, my good Klyne, Otto says.

Suicide? Christenze says. I'll make it easy for her.

Otto gets up. He goes over to a small table and pours himself a glass of red wine, then raises his glass to the others:

I give you His Majesty King Christian IV, by the Grace of God King of all Denmark and Norway, the Goths and the Wends, Duke of Schleswig, Holstein, Stormarn and Ditmarsh, Count of Oldenburg and Delmenhorst. God bless him!

He dashes the glass to the floor, and it shatters. They give a collective start.

Can I have some? Pour a little for me, Klyne says.

Otto pours each of them a glass.

What is it you have there? Elisabeth tries tentatively.

It is the doll Karen gave me, Christenze replies.

They drink in silence to still their nerves.

There is a stirring at the entrance. The king appears, blindfolded. He has been engaged in a game of blind man's buff in the adjoining hall and waves back at the courtiers. The bench is emptied immediately, clothes straightened, Christenze lifts her chest. A moment then, when they can see the king, but he cannot see them.

Is that him? Elisabeth whispers.

Shh! Otto hisses, we are not allowed to speak until he has addressed us.

Is anyone there? the king says playfully.

Glances are exchanged, should they answer? His Majesty approaches.

Yoo-hooo, is anyone there? Come out, come out, wherever you are!

No one speaks. Then, from Christenze's mouth, a little girl's voice answers:

Tee-hee, yes, someone is here.

Otto gesticulates silently for her to stop.

Then here I come to gobble you up! says Christian IV.

Without a sound Christenze slips behind Otto. The girl's laughter returns. Otto clears his throat.

Your Majesty, he ventures.

Ah, there's another one! the king exclaims.

The little girl's voice inside Christenze says:

A big fat fart!

The king steps forward, his hands grope Klyne.

Good day, good day, says the blind one. And who have we here?

With a big smile he pinches and pulls at Klyne's face, as if kneading dough. Klyne appears so utterly shocked and in awe that he can only let it happen.

Is it an old woman? the king asks.

Then Otto ventures again:

Your Majesty. Allow me to introduce myself . . .

But the king ignores him and instead asks the room another question:

Doggy, where are you?

Christenze is on all fours behind Otto and sticks her head out between his legs to answer the king. Her little girl's voice is replaced by the French she learned when she was young:

Me voici, Votre Majesté.

The king reaches for the voice but Christenze jerks her head back and instead the king finds his hand full of Otto's genitals. Otto flinches, humiliated, but still he attempts to stay in character, saying nothing. It is not only discomfort in Otto's face as he is felt up by the monarch. Christenze runs through the hall, but the king is quick, he follows and catches her, and shakes her vigorously.

Got you, you little piggy!

She tries to pry herself loose, but cannot.

Who is your king? the king says.

You are, Your Majesty.

Both are huffing. The light that falls through the leaded

panes is like drinking water. There is a taste of tin and chalk. Christenze and the king stand close together. She pulls the blindfold from his eyes. Her mouth is near his.

You have no idea who I am, have you?

Yes, I do, he replies.

Who, then?

You are the Jomfru Christenze, the one who holds the skin girdle the longest.

Do you know why I am here?

Yes, I do.

Will you let me live?

No, he says.

The game is over. He releases her. Christenze stands as if made of stone. No one says a word. The king motions, his guards enter and she is taken away. Where she stood, I lie, the wax child. I fell from one of her deep pockets during the chase. Elisabeth runs over and quickly picks me up, carries me like a living child on her arm.

Are you a bad one too? the king asks.

Me? Elisabeth replies. I am no more than a little bee that flies away.

It is early morning, the twenty-sixth of June 1621. On Gammeltorv, the execution place is being prepared, the mood is light, the people work well together. It is clear by the fluidity of their movements that they have done this all before and are familiar. A sword is wiped, a hangman's hood then worn, a lined basket positioned for the head. The residents of the city fill the square. In the surrounding houses windows are opened. Now Christenze comes walking along Skindergade. She is wearing a smock, or underwear.

They see it all, Klyne, Otto, and next to them Elisabeth. She cannot grasp it. Everyone is talking, but they emit no sound. A loneliness courses through her and cools her blood.

Someone steps forward and reads aloud the sentence:

Jomfru Christenze Axelsdatter Kruckow has committed inadmissible deeds. She has issued threats against upstanding citizens and promised them misfortune. By her own admission, she has written upon confessional wafers and given them to sick people to eat. She has been denounced by numerous witches, who for their despicable deeds have been sentenced to death in Funen and North Jutland. These witches have told that she was with them in society and in company. She has been unable to deny these deeds to the court, nor to disprove or cast doubt over them or even the smallest matter for which she stands charged. Jomfru Christenze Axelsdatter Kruckow is found guilty of having performed unlawful and unchristian acts. In so doing, she has offended against her own noble standing and dignity, and shall hereby be sentenced to her death. However, in view that she is of noble family, she shall instead of burning be executed by the sword.

The king has arrived at the place of execution.

As we are gathered here today, our kingdom is in great peril, he says, for the depth of the Devil's malice matches only with his madness, he says. Some will be timid in the face of witchcraft and shrink from action. Make no mistake, your King will act. Witches are nourished by a terrible evil and wish only to subvert God's creation. They cast sickness upon their enemies, steal the body parts of good men, and devour innocent children. Know that your King will do whatever is necessary to ensure the safety of the realm. None of us would wish that evil be among us. But the witch before us today is proof that these milk-maids of the Devil are everywhere to be found. Every citizen of the Danish realm now has a decision to make: either stand with God and your King, or stand with the Devil and his witches. Let the Lord himself be our witness. Today, Denmark is cleansed of a terrible witch.

The king's head turns, he is silent now and waiting.

I see her tremble at the sword. Swallows twitter. There is a daytime moon. The smell of seaweed from the stagnant canals swims over us. In the cells, prisoners listen for the chop, for the wet sound of the throat's interior exposed. She screams, and the scream is like a whistle. There is a gurgling and a creaking from a yard pump giving water. Then a small fire is lit, and the head and body of the deceased are tossed upon it so as to ensure that the witch cannot rise again. It is Saturday. Church-bells chime. The execution is done. Onlookers amble away through the streets in small groups. Eventually, only Elisabeth remains. The fire burns. She turns her back on it. The image of Maren's hand flashes through her and Apelone's laughter, Dorte there at her maternity bed. A crackling sound, a heaviness, comes over her, as if the wind has been knocked out of her.

Behind her, Christenze's head rolls out of the fire. The head opens its mouth and emits a dry gargle, a snore almost, though the eyes are wide open. The head speaks:

When I was a little girl, my father took me down to see the horses. It was a blue day, I think, I was seven or eight, and the world lived inside me like dithering air, and I assumed that everything had but a single name and a single truth to it, and that all the truths had to be learned by heart; that the world was merely one long list of unambiguous names. It is a mystery to me how I became the person I became, a heart of wax on a hook. Did I love sufficiently? Fiercely enough? So soft the bluebell's leaves behind the castle wall when I was a child. So cool the mirror of the blade when held against my cheek and teeming with life were my thighs. I believe I am magnificent. Now through the fire I see a glade, and there a girl leads a she-goat towards the forest, its udder taut with milk. A she-goat for milking! Although I do not know the future, I see it. The reason is behind us. All reasons are behind us. The fire has its own reason. The future is already visible. It is over there by the exits. I want you to look directly into the fire. But it will not happen. The fire has gone out. We are not even here. We have been here.

You will hear me in the night under the breath of your sleeping children. You will hear me when spring turns to summer, and there in the light an opening occurs, Elisabeth, will you come with us to the Lucia fest, Elisabeth? Magic is possible. Laughter is possible. There is a way out, Elisabeth, there is a way out . . .

What sweet and muddled words my mistress said there. I saw Elisabeth tuck up her skirt and put her hands into its fabric. I saw her thus with protected hands lift the glowing-hot head. I saw her toss the head into the gutter and kick it, so that it could be carried away.

Had I eyes that could weep, I would have wept. But I am only a doll, a child of wax. I cannot move my hands. My wax mouth cannot be opened. And yet I speak. How is it possible? I can sing very well, like a bird at the top of a birch tree. To the dead I mean nothing. I meant little to them when they were alive. To my mistress I was only an instrument. Made for strength, made for harm. I am so stupid. Every evening I tell the same story, and I speak to the soil.

AUTHOR'S NOTE

This novel was written on top of Nordic folklore as well as a large number of historical sources – letters, ledgers, court documents and theological texts – most of them concerning witch trials that took place in northern Europe.

The spells that occur at intervals throughout the novel stem entirely from so-called black books, grimoires and other such works, sometimes bearing the name Cyprianus, dating variously to the period 1400 to 1900. To make them more accessible to a modern reader, I have adapted the original wordings somewhat, while in a number of cases different versions of the same spell have been combined. Many are taken from original handwritten sources kept at the Royal Danish Library in Copenhagen and the Trolldomsarkivet at the University of Oslo.

The events described, and the names of the various characters, come from a series of Danish witch trials that took place in Funen (Danish: Fyn) and in Aalborg, North Jutland, between 1596 and 1621.

In real life, the Aalborg case extended over a period of some ten years, but events have been condensed here – so a mention of something taking place in 1620 or 1621 might actually mean anywhere between 1611 and 1621. Besides the women mentioned, a woman from southern Funen and three women of Aalborg were also found guilty of witchcraft and subsequently executed in connection with the cases surrounding Christenze Kruckow. Some of their names do appear fleetingly in the novel, but all should be properly mentioned here:

> Johanne Jensen, Nakkebølle, burned on an unknown date, probably in 1597.
> Mette Pedersdatter, Aalborg, burned 1612.
> Maren Pedersdatter, Aalborg, burned 3 February 1620.
> Elle Nielsdatter, Aalborg, burned late summer 1620.

The actual dates of death for the five women in the novel are as follows:

> Ousse Lauridsdatter, Nakkebølle, burned on an unknown date, probably in 1597.
> Maren Kneppis, Aalborg, burned 1612.
> Apelone Ibsdatter, Aalborg, burned 29 or 30 October 1619.
> Dorte Kjærulf, Aalborg, burned 1620.
> Christenze Kruckow, Copenhagen, beheaded 26 June 1621.

A number of other women appear by name in court documents concerning the Aalborg trials, but then disappear from them without further mention. It seems reasonable to believe that some of these women died while proceedings were ongoing, perhaps in captivity, perhaps by suicide, but the archives provide no definitive answers.

ACKNOWLEDGEMENTS

First and foremost, I'm hugely grateful to everyone involved in the theatre production *HEX*, which premiered at the Royal Danish Theatre on 28 April 2023. This novel builds on that play, dialoguing with the script I wrote for it. Particular thanks are due to Liv Helm for her keen, bold and sensitive readings and suggestions.

Thanks also to Freya Sif Hestnes, Jeanett Albeck and Benedikte Hammershøy Nielsen, to all the cast, musicians and crew, and to the theatre itself.

Additionally, I'm greatly indebted to Ida Simone Bzorek and Signe Buchgraitz Jensen, who helped me source and decipher original documents relating to the court case. Mette Kierstein was an invaluable researcher and sparring partner along the way. Thanks to Tom Silkeberg, Niels Henning Krag Jensby, Johanne Lykke Naderehvandi, Morten Chemnitz, Mette Mortensen and Simon Pasternak. Thanks to Hanne Fabricius, who helped plot Christenze's route through Copenhagen, and to churchyard officer Annee Katrine Bonde at Sønderholm Kirkegård, who, although our efforts were in vain, accompanied me in trying to locate Christenze's grave. Thanks to Nanna Hovgaard and Josephine Kuhn for driving me around Aalborg and surroundings, and for being hospitable and accommodating. Thanks to Harald Voetmann for his anecdotes about Christian IV, for manning the swallow-stone hotline, and for pointing out the connection between Manderup Parsberg and Tycho Brahe. Thanks to Louise Kallestrup for so kindly responding to even my weirdest questions about matters great and small. Thanks to Poul Grinder-Hansen and Clara Dalsgaard of the National Museum of Denmark for going through the manuscript from a historical perspective. Finally, I'd like to thank three people who for some or all of the way accompanied me in researching the accused women: Ruth Storm, Ulrikke Neergaard and Fulya Erdemci.

In addition to the sources mentioned above, the novel obliquely references the following poems: 'Advent' by Gillian Clarke, 'Detail of the Woods' by Richard Siken and 'The Glass Essay' by Anne Carson, as well as the song 'Björnen' by Sara Parkman.